S0-AVS-533

"The pace, while leisurely, never flags, and Gross establishes credible relationships in a vivid New York setting, holding promise for future Maggie Van Zandt stories."
—*Publishers Weekly* on *Full Blown Rage*

"Intricate weave of counterplots.... First-rate melodrama, with just enough resonance to make you see how far out past their depth Jack and Bonnie are."
—*Kirkus Reviews* on *Full Blown Rage*

"Gross's panorama of backroom Gotham politics is so exuberant that Jack and Bonnie's routine investigation of the inevitable homicides, when the plot finally kicks in, comes as something of a letdown: you wish these guys could go on stabbing each other in the back, like Dante's sinners, for all eternity."
—*Kirkus Reviews* on *A High Pressure System*

"This is an odd mix of breezy, brash detecting; a trendy setting; and a gore-filled dose of murder and mayhem— victims seem to have particularly bad luck with getting their eyes poked out. The plot is consistently over the top...but Van Zandt manages to keep events from totally spinning into the stratosphere. Recommended for those who like their mysteries both light and dark."
—*Booklist* on *The Talk Show Defense*

"A lively tale that packs more than its share of twists before settling into the inevitable mano a mano between Maggie and her prey."
—*Kirkus Reviews* on *The Talk Show Defense*

THE TALK SHOW
DEFENSE

KEN GROSS

TOR®

A TOM DOHERTY ASSOCIATES BOOK
NEW YORK

This is a work of fiction. All the characters and events portrayed in this book are either products of the author's imagination or are used fictitiously.

THE TALK SHOW DEFENSE

Copyright © 1997 by Ken Gross

A Tor Book
Published by Tom Doherty Associates, LLC
175 Fifth Avenue
New York, NY 10010

www.tor.com

Tor® is a registered trademark of Tom Doherty Associates, LLC.

ISBN: 0-812-55025-0
Library of Congress Catalog Card Number: 96-53529

First edition: May 1997
First mass market edition: October 2000

Printed in the United States of America

0 9 8 7 6 5 4 3 2 1

To Emily and Melanie,
grand children;
and Arnie "Doc" Schwartz

THE TALK SHOW

DEFENSE

PROLOGUE

TUESDAY, JANUARY 10

Peggy O'Neill was met in the lobby of the Global Television Network by a pair of extravagantly solicitous young women. They wore concerned smiles and bent very close, taking Peggy by the elbows as if she were an invalid. They brought her up to the fifth-floor backstage offices in a reserved elevator, chatting incessantly about how easy this whole business was going to be. They offered her coffee and sweet rolls and bathed her in an atmosphere of such lavish care and sympathy that she was filled with a paralyzing sense of dread.

As they walked down a narrow corridor lined with oversized photographs of smiling in-house television stars, Peggy thought about backing out. But it no longer seemed possible. The physical momentum of advancing down the hall seemed to make each step irreversible.

The escorts took her into the greenroom. It was small and brightly lit and cluttered. There was a makeup table in front of a mirrored wall. Against the far wall there was a long couch, and above the couch was a collection of nine-by-twelve-inch photographs of celebrity guests with their autographs and yearbook sentiments.

The young women hovered over Peggy, who sat on the couch

while they waited for the senior production assistant, who would go through the essential preshow interview. And sitting there, Peggy could not help but be aware of the contrast between herself and the young women. In their careless denim jeans and college sweatshirts, her escorts exuded a pitch of jaunty confidence and glowed with high promise. In her shapeless coat and mud-dull hat, Peggy O'Neill felt dim and drab and cringed with misgivings and shame.

"Mr. Lock is on the way," assured the Dartmouth girl, who handed Peggy a blue mug marked *The Kevin Grant Show* and a wooden stick to stir the packets of sugar into the coffee, and then touched her hand gently. The Harvard girl placed a plastic plate with a prune danish on a coffee table in front of the couch. She folded a napkin next to it. They were like golden, Ivy League airline stewardesses, thought Peggy.

Then the door opened and in came the senior production assistant, Gary Lock. He was a stocky young man with a thinning crew cut. He wore a *Kevin Grant Show* T-shirt and carried a clipboard. The two young women quickly left the room.

"This is very, very good of you," said Gary Lock, laying down his clipboard and holding out his hand, which was nail-bitten and small and surprisingly soft.

Peggy laughed nervously. "I don't know what I'm doing here," she said.

The senior production assistant took a chair and pulled it close to Peggy O'Neill. He leaned over, holding her hand cupped in his own, and spoke in a half whisper.

"You are doing a brave, brave thing," he said.

She laughed again.

"You know, there are a lot of women out there who are going through the same sort of thing," he said softly. "Women whose husbands cheat. Women whose husbands abuse them. What you are doing is giving them all a big shot of courage. The courage to do what you have done."

"All I did was get divorced," she replied.

He reached behind him, took the clipboard from the

makeup table, and began the preinterview. He looked down at the notes. The mood became a little more clinical.

"No," replied Gary Lock. "You stood up to an abusive husband. You refused to be a victim."

"You know, I'm not really sure that I can talk about it."

He put his pencil down and gazed deeply into her eyes. "Of course you can. Look, Peggy, this show is a story. There will be other women on the stage with you. Your story and their stories are important. There are thousands and thousands of similar stories in America today. We have to honestly tell that story. Your husband was abusive and unfaithful."

She nodded. "He was," she said.

Gary nodded emphatically, picking up his pencil and making notes on a card on the clipboard.

"We can't turn our backs on that," he said. "That was a terrible thing."

"Yes, it was."

"Somewhere, someone has to draw a line in the sand."

She nodded. "I can't tell you how many times I had to call the police."

He looked into her eyes again. "I know that there had to be times when you wanted to get even. Get back a little of your own, as my mother would say."

She laughed.

"This show is—in a small way—getting back a little of their own for thousands and thousands of abused women. It is a kind of justice."

"Well . . ."

He laughed. "Look, I know what I would do if I had been through what you've been through. I'm not being presumptuous. I'm just saying I know what I'd do."

"What?"

"I'd go out there and tell the whole world what was done to me. Like you, I'd refuse to be a victim." He shook his head. "No way are you a victim."

She nodded. Yes, she could say what had to be said, when

it was put in those terms. She had been a victim. But no more.

"You were abused," he continued, shaking his head.

"Yes," she said. Peggy's cheeks had come to life with the possibility of a small revenge.

"This is fighting back."

"Well, it's not exactly fighting back." She laughed, feeling easier now, experiencing an expanding self-possession. "All I did was to get out of the marriage. The score isn't quite evened up. There were so many . . . There were women who actually called my home! I think that bothered me more than the beatings!"

Gary Lock nodded, then shook his head. "You know what else I'd do to that son of a bitch? I'd go out there and say, 'Yes, I was beaten, yes, he cheated on me, and you know what? I had a little bit of a fling myself. I cheated right back at him!' That would really fix his wagon! That would be justice."

She laughed. "Oh, that would get him, all right. That would get him really crazy."

"So? Didn't he make you crazy? Did he care about you?"

"Yes, but you don't know Mickey."

"Oh, maybe I don't know Mickey, but I know his type. Big man. Big talk. What can he do? You're on television. He can't hurt you, not when everybody's seen you. You think he could touch you after that?" He shook his head.

She asked, "But you can't say something that's not true. Can you?"

He snorted. "What's the difference? Who would know?" He looked up from his notes again. "I'm not telling you what to do. I'm only saying what I'd do."

There was a long moment of silence. An intern poked his head through the door and said that they had ten minutes until the show and that Gary had to brief Kevin Grant.

"I couldn't," she said when the intern closed the door behind him.

"I'll tell you one thing: It would make every woman watching stand up and cheer. That whole studio audience will stand up and cheer."

She shook her head.

He shrugged. "But that would be me. I'm only saying what I'd do."

When he left the greenroom and the makeup artist came in, she thought about it. The idea swam through her brain and she was dizzy with the possibility.

But she couldn't think it through. They came for her before she was ready. The urgency and panic were contagious. Everything was done in a TV delirium. Staff people grabbed her arm and moved her out of the room as if she were a prop. Because she was a delicate prop that required some handling, they whispered harsh, insincere encouragement. She was propelled breathlessly down intense corridors and through hectic groups. Finally she found herself on the set, in a great open space, and felt the blast of the live audience and the muzzle of the cameras.

A stage manager told her the rules of the show—when to speak, when to listen—but she didn't comprehend. Someone pinned a microphone to her collar and she submitted helplessly. Peggy sat on a tall wooden stool, perched unsteadily under the burning sun of the high-intensity lights, tracked by the hard, appraising eyes of the cameras. Then the host emerged from behind a curtain. She was shocked by the sight of Kevin Grant. He was older than she expected—her father's age. Before she was ready the show had begun. She watched Kevin Grant prowling up and down in front of her, his eyes empty of interest. And she found herself speaking. The words came out like something launched from her throat—a piece of meat for the hungry audience. But in the end, no matter how hard she pitched her case, she experienced the sinking certainty of diminishing interest.

An hour later, Peggy walked out of the studio and into the Manhattan winter afternoon. There was no one at her side. The consoling young women had gone off to comfort someone else.

Her mind was a blur. She didn't remember the show clearly. She didn't remember what she said, only the howling wind inside her head as she had plunged ahead, saying wild, intoxicated things that she never meant to say. She had been blinded and frozen dumb by the lights and the cameras and the painful need to please and prolong her television life. She had said whatever came into her head.

It was not enough. Shortly after it began, Kevin Grant had turned his lifeless eyes to another, more interesting guest, terminating the interview. He had grown bored with Peggy O'Neill.

She knew, even behind the shade of her temporary amnesia, that she had lied. Even if she couldn't reconstruct the whole interview as she walked from Sixty-seventh Street to Fifty-ninth Street, she was aware that she had gone way too far.

But then it came to her—bleeding back into her memory, word by word—after she boarded the "N" train back to Queens. And when she reached the point when she recalled saying that she had gotten even with her unfaithful and abusive husband, Mickey, by having an extramarital love affair, she put her face in her hands and wept. No one on the subway paid attention.

ONE

On the morning after her television confession, Peggy O'Neill was five minutes late for work.

Her boss, Mel Carr, was standing at the window of the storefront LAW OFFICE in the outer borough of Queens, squinting through the printed letter *O*, wondering which version of Peggy O'Neill would come through the front door—the shy little thing who kept his office tidy, or the tainted TV guest who had shocked ten million viewers.

He didn't blame himself for Peggy's outburst, although technically he was responsible for her appearance on the talk show. However, after more than forty years of practicing a kind of urban frontier law out of his Queens office, Mel Carr had perfected the art of shifting blame. His clients were never solely at fault for the foul laundry list of misdeeds laid at their feet by the police. No matter how red-handed they were caught, no matter how heinous the act, no matter how incriminating the circumstances, the offenses themselves always had another sinister root. Blame a rotten upbringing, blame a malicious criminal-justice system, blame a conspiracy of fate. Blame everyone but the client.

As for Peggy O'Neill, how, he asked, deflecting a phantom accusation, could he have forseen the eruption?

Well, the truth was that he always suspected something. Mel Carr suspected the worst from everyone who came through the soiled and fortified front door of his office. Peggy O'Neill was no exception.

Finally, having stood at the window for fifteen minutes, shifting from one foot to the other, he spotted Peggy making her way to work. In spite of every cause for alarm, he smiled. Peggy O'Neill was floundering on the traffic island that divided Queens Boulevard into six lanes, her head bobbing and weaving as the cars flashed by like waves of attacking bayonets. She had returned to her usual state of benign confusion.

So the eruption—if that's what it was—was nothing more than a pseudoevent, a technoglich in an otherwise sound and functioning personality. She had undergone a television-induced outburst, like a reflexive wave of a hand at a tragic crime scene. And now she had put herself back together.

From this distance he couldn't see her pale, lumpy features, but he didn't have to. She was wearing the familiar shapeless winter coat, along with the heavy, mud-dull woolen hat (a hat Mel Carr believed—with pure visionary clarity—would one day ring down over her face like a final curtain). He also knew with heart-breaking certainty that she was, at this very moment, going through her standard emotional stammer; Peggy O'Neill was one of those people caught forever between an uncertain smile and unspoken grief. There was never an unclouded moment of her life when the poor woman knew whether to laugh or cry.

Or, at least, that was Mel Carr's fixed opinion, which, like many of his quick convictions, was a bad miscalculation. His views were based on his own brittle inability to take into account the possibility of change, never mind more subtle prospects. Mel Carr was defiantly obstinate about his own first impressions. No one changed—they merely acted with variations on his original assumptions. This faith was only a slight modification on his cement avoidance of blame.

Nevertheless, he was anxious about the mental state of his receptionist. He nursed a small stone of guilt rolling around his belly. For his own greedy purposes, Mel Carr had volunteered her as a guest on the afternoon talk show.

It could be viewed as an example of his own elementary weakness. When the talk show's booker called and asked if he knew someone with personal experience in an abusive marriage, Mel had suggested himself. Certainly not as an abusive partner (he was a widower), but as an expert in the field. He had spent all that time as a general-practice lawyer operating out of a Queens storefront; that certainly qualified him for a postgraduate degree on the marital martial arts. The television booker on the other end of the phone didn't even bother to answer Mel's offer, just waited in that airless pocket of deep, insulting silence until Mel absorbed the truth—they didn't want him. They wanted a suffering victim. And so he offered up Peggy.

As he suspected, Peggy didn't want to do it; but Mel was the boss and among all the other obligations that came attached with steel strings, she owed him money for handling her divorce. Mel Carr ignored her apparent misery, then tried another tack. Oh, never mind, he said finally; if you really don't want to do it . . . He would just call and break the already offered promise. Never mind the cost. Forget about it. He even seemed to soften, as if her pain carried some weight in his calculations.

And then he went into his rear office and shut the door, pretending that he was truly making that humiliating phone call to cancel the appearance. In fact, he just sat there, holding the telephone receiver in a theatrical pose of action. Finally, as he knew that she would, Peggy knocked softly, came slouched and repentant into his office, and agreed to do the show. She never had any real choice.

The next day, subdued by a fresh dress—plus five milligrams of Valium (donated by Mel Carr)—Peggy O'Neill went on the show and declared that in retaliation for years of her husband's

philandering and drunken brutality, she, too, had been unfaithful.

It didn't really explode on television—hers was just one more
shameless personal confession of human frailty—but watching
at home, it froze Mel Carr. She was gone from the set after a commercial break. Either she was too overwrought to continue or
she didn't have enough talk-show sizzle—he couldn't tell. Another woman, a victim with fresh homegrown bruises, sat in her
chair.

It was just television, he told himself. Part of the endless
scroll of afternoon misery. But Mel Carr recognized the sound
of authentic sorrow in Peggy's voice. In fact, he thought about
it all night long. Somewhere, in that little pink moment before
dawn, as he lay brooding about it, Mel Carr found an excuse for
her: Peggy O'Neill was a child. It had escaped him, what with her
middle-aged bearing and heavyhearted manner, but his receptionist was still in her late twenties! She might appear mature and
competent beyond her years, but it was all an act of will. She was
only prematurely mature. He remembered the date of birth on
her divorce papers. She was still a child.

As he stood at the storefront window waiting for her to navigate
the traffic, Mel Carr twisted his head and bent himself sideways
to see if he could find a fresh perspective on this strange, vacil-
lating woman, bobbing like a cork between the dueling cars and
trucks and buses. He tried to see if, perhaps, from this grimy
peephole in the painted sign, he could detect some hint of the
other woman, the one capable of using ancient and spiteful
means of revenge; someone who could—as was the modern,
crude practice—defiantly proclaim her intimate sexual secret on
television.

"You never know," he said to the shatterproof glass contained
behind the wire mesh screen. Mel Carr was sixty-three years old.
A plain, storefront lawyer. His was a rough practice. Eighteen-B.
Court-appointed cases. Every working day he inhaled the foul,

unsentimental air of criminal cunning. The people who sat on his frayed couch and broken chairs in a presentencing daze were strung-out junkies, hopeless burglars, doomed street hustlers, unfeeling gang-bangers. Some came to his office accompanied by crestfallen parents who listened in stunned gloom to the long menu of consequences. Some came dangling neon brides. Some came alone. They all had dull, dead eyes that beheld no worthwhile destination.

It was a draining thing to confront so much spoiled humanity, and over the years Mel Carr had developed tactics to protect himself against excessive direct contact with the clients. He put a receptionist out front. Always, Mel Carr found a sympathetic soul to act as a shatterproof emotional window against all the ill winds that blew through his waiting room.

On the traffic island, Peggy glanced back and forth, looking for a break in the flash of cars. She carried in her arms the usual cargo of flowers and home-baked cakes. Once again, Mel Carr was touched. Even after a great emotional train wreck, she still managed the small acts of daily grace. She still baked cakes and bought fresh flowers for the office.

A creature of reliable, unselfish habits. That's what he first concluded when he hired her six months earlier. It was against the preference of his partner, Benny Stern, who wanted someone young and brassy to make an explosive first impression.

No, Carr had said finally, after coolly considering the assortment of candidates. He didn't want the bored high-school graduates, or the social worker-ants. This one, he told Benny Stern, referring to Peggy, is a nester. She will build a tidy sanctuary out of her cold metal desk and the surrounding gray cabinets; she will transform our dreary little office into something almost cozy.

And so she did. With her modest feats of thoughtfulness she turned the plain storefront law office of Mel Carr and Benny Stern into a haven, which is what Mel required when so many clients arrived in a state of legal shock.

Peggy O'Neill—always fighting off colds and migraines—had just lost a job working in a pharmacy that had gone out of business, and she was suited to a fastidious work ethic. She moved into the law office and swept her desk clean hourly and made little Post-it notes about people's birthdays and anniversaries and began a meticulous update of the dog-eared and chaotic Rolodex. She dusted the blinds and made certain that there were fresh towels in the washrooms.

It went without saying that Peggy's refuge was constructed out of cast-off twigs and dross. But, fresh from her own divorce, the underpaid receptionist needed a home. (That, too, went into Mel Carr's calculations.) He felt vindicated. Her presence transformed the stark, quick-fix atmosphere of the office, gave it the illusion of substance, of place. The boxes of buns and doughnuts, along with pots of freshly brewed coffee, were offered to all the troubled clients who came through the door of Carr and Stern seeking miracle legal cures.

Even so, she had been nothing more to Mel Carr than a plain piece of office furniture. A switch that he threw to turn on a light. But after that talk show, he had to rethink his attitude. It appeared that his docile and domesticated receptionist could be someone with moist, erotic dimensions.

Peggy found a break between the cars and pressed on with a sailor's wobbly step. She came through the door quickly and, as she always did, went straight to work, putting away her things in the closet, fluffing the flowers in the vases, arranging the cakes on a large platter, cleaning out the coffeepot. The only difference was the blotches of red on her skin showing the high, agitated undercoating of her state of mind. Mel Carr smiled at her the way he smiled at juries—as if they shared a deep, guilty secret.

"Peggy," he began, but when she looked up and met his eyes, he saw something new. She pushed him away with her stare. Then, in a voice that he did not recognize, something that she had held back, she spoke. "You know, the funny thing is, I wanted to do that show."

"I don't know what to say."

She turned back to her things, her duties, the routine activities, moving papers pointlessly around the desk.

"Well, what's done is done," she said in a tall, trembling voice that rose like smoke.

That must be the operating consolation of her life, Mel Carr thought. What's done is done. He went over to the pot and poured her a cup of coffee.

"Are you all right?" he asked.

She sunk her face into the cup of coffee, then looked up and smiled weakly. "I think Mickey may be worse."

Mel Carr nodded. He thought about the husband. Ex-husband. Chunky little man losing all his hair, angry at the world over the consumption of his youth, his life, his hair. Ready to punch all the time; that was what Mel Carr thought when they met and the little man put out his fist. He was relieved when it unrolled into an open handshake. But it could have been a punch. It would have made very little difference to Mickey O'Neill if he slammed you with his fist or offered up his handshake, thought Mel Carr. He would have had the exact same mean little squint in his eyes.

"Oh, he didn't see the show," said Carr, with the same tone of false confidence he used when he told convicted felons that he would get right to work on an appeal. "He wouldn't watch that kind of show. And that segment—it went by very fast."

She smiled, knew the trick. "You know," she began, then stopped, looked up, had that half smile of sorrow on her face, and said, "the funniest part . . . it wasn't even true."

He paused and looked at her, and then back at his coffee. He didn't get it. What was she talking about? What wasn't true? He looked around, as if there were some explanation in some other part of the room. "What are you talking about?"

"The thing I said. I never . . . Never!" Then she barked a laugh. "I couldn't. Not that it wasn't deserved . . . But it wasn't true."

He did not comprehend. "You mean . . . ?"

She nodded. "I mean—there was no other man." She rolled her head and laughed again. It was a snarling laugh. "I couldn't do such a thing."

She nodded emphatically. A truth. He had coached enough witnesses in the telling of sworn lies that he could recognize the truth.

"So . . . then . . . why did you say it?"

She shrugged. Just a rise and fall of the shoulders, as if such things came and went. "Someone . . . said it would be a good way to get even," she said finally. "It didn't mean anything. It didn't have to be true—who would ever know the difference?"

She smiled pathetically.

"They told you to say that?"

She was not one to shift blame. "They didn't tell me. They suggested the possibility."

"I don't understand."

"It really doesn't make any difference, you know." There was a long drop of fatalism in her voice. She sensed his prosecutorial direction. "I said it. It was me. I just said it. Now let's just forget it."

They both spun away from each other, faced another surface—a change of scene to reconsider, to look somewhere else—and their gaze turned simultaneously to the window. At that instant, they both saw Mickey O'Neill. He was running and puffing across the boulevard. The cars swerved and hit their brakes and avoided the collision. He didn't seem to care if he was hit. A heedless, dangerous sight.

Mel felt a sudden spasm of alarm. "You want me to call the police?"

She shook her head with resignation. She got up. She seemed unusually calm. "I'll handle it," she said without hope.

Mel Carr went into his private office and turned on the intercom. He toyed with the idea of dialing 911. He decided to wait. Then he became an audience as Peggy and Mickey glared at each other. Mel's ears burned, and he looked to see where the phone rested in case he had to make that quick emergency call. He couldn't hear whatever it was that they uttered under their breaths to each other. When he looked up he saw Peggy take her coat and her mud-dull hat and march out of the office with her ex-husband.

As he watched them crossing Queens Boulevard, brazen against the onslaught of traffic, Mel Carr came up with an idea, should it ever come to that. It was cold-blooded but shrewd. Either way, he would call it "the talk-show defense." A lawsuit. A criminal tactic. It didn't matter. He could already see the tabloid headline.

TWO

Mickey O'Neill drove with his jaw clenched and his right hand free to swat sideways at his ex-wife, Peggy, who cowered on the passenger side of the old pickup truck, just out of reach. He made ferocious circles through the Sunnyside and Long Island City neighborhoods, racing up streets with dead factories at the end, then wheeling around in a screaming K-turn, heading back onto Northern Boulevard, the spine of the borough of Queens. The dented and rusted pickup truck duplicated the stammering movements of the driver's aroused and convulsive temper.

When they had an easy stretch of straightaway, Mickey reached over and took another swipe at his ex-wife. "Bitch!" he cried, an oath that so understated the extent of his fury that it took on added, weightier meaning. Then, suddenly, they were on the girded birdcage of the Queensboro Bridge, heading toward Manhattan. And all the while Mickey didn't speak, merely articulated disjointed grunts and howls of hot rage.

Peggy had a combat veteran's calm terror in the face of her ex-husband's outburst. After all, she had been through wild domestic wars before. She knew all there was to know about male anger. She had spent a lifetime enduring it, dodging it, and, finally, deflecting it. And it didn't start with a bad marriage. From her earliest childhood, Peggy could remember nights when she lay shivering in her bed, waiting in dread until her stepfather got through beating her mother. Shamefully, she wanted the beatings to go on. The longer they went on, the greater the chance that he would get tired and fall into a spent stupor. Even if he didn't stop, it was enough that her turn would be postponed by a long pounding. Even a few extra moments were something to prize.

Within that insane loop of guilt, she suffered in a withering, brutal home, knowing the exact price her mother was paying for her own stay of execution. Sooner or later, her stepfather would come into her room. He would loom over her bed and she would listen to his labored, whiskey breathing as he waited to strike.

There were nights when he would simply grab her by the hair and yank her right out of her bed without warning, flinging her up against the plasterboard walls of their slum apartment, shattering glass and breaking furniture. The family dwelled within the splintered wreckage of savage emotions and poor possessions.

From then on, Peggy O'Neill understood the exact calculus of abuse. She had, with cold clarity, estimated the price of turning against her stepfather. Naturally, she could not physically oppose him, but she could report him to the authorities. It would carve up the family, turn mother against child, snap whatever links persisted in that depraved chain. She had to consider that. Even a dysfunctional, abusive family was better than the unimaginable and unthinkable chaos of a nomadic, homeless existence on the street. Better to absorb the abuse, until that moment when it became unbearable, whenever that moment revealed itself.

To escape, she married the first man who came along. He happened to be another brute, and the calculations changed slightly. If she called the police on Mickey, he swore that he would kill her. He would spend some time in jail, but then he would be released and he would find her, no matter where she was, and murder her. When he explained this to her, in a demonically calm and businesslike way, she had no doubt that he meant what he said, and she absolutely believed him.

And so, with mathematical precision, she assessed each kick and punch and threat, balancing them against the possibility of a successful break for freedom. She computed the known risk of murder against a remote emancipation. It was a tricky thing. Finally, she found a way to leave Mickey without provoking a lethal attack. She became a burden. She suffered one nervous breakdown after another. In the end, he was glad to get rid of her.

But that was earlier, without the added factor of a grievous wound to his ego. That was before she went on television and announced that she had turned him into a cuckold. And now, as she recoiled in the cab of the pickup truck ducking his thick fists, she tried to recalculate her options.

"It was a lie," she tried to plead. "The thing I said on television was a lie."

"Lying bitch!" he replied, lunging across the cab and hitting her crossed, battered arms.

"No!" she swore. "I never had an affair. It was something that they made up. To make the program more interesting."

She was screaming and he was screaming, and the words were a blend of incomprehensible fury and fear. They heard only their own wretched cries.

Mickey drove erratically up First Avenue. He parked the pickup truck on 110th Street in Spanish Harlem, on a block of ruined tenements and hopeless addicts. Walking, they passed a storefront needle exchange clinic, and she could see the tribe of jitterbug junkies dancing restlessly from foot to foot in the cold as they waited to make the switch of dirty needles for clean works. Mickey didn't notice the street traffic as he dragged Peggy west and downtown. But she could tell, as they moved quickly through the streets, that he was thinking about what she said. She could sense a shift in the murderous atmosphere.

"Why'd you do it?" he asked angrily.

He had stopped. They were somewhere in the nineties on an empty street. She could see blinds shift in the windows as tenants peeked at the event. She welcomed Mickey's question. Maybe it meant something besides blind violence.

"I swear, I was only saying what they told me to say."

He grabbed her arm and she could feel the fingers digging in through the cloth. It was as if he were trying to strangle her arm. Now he would kill her, she thought. Now that they were strangers in a strange part of town, where people peeked out of the windows and then hid from involvement. He pulled her, heading to the park. She decided that if they passed a cop, she would scream. She had nothing left to lose.

They stopped at a deli and he bought beer and sandwiches. They ate the food on the street, then wandered, losing track of time.

But they didn't pass a cop, and he came to a decision and jerked her along until they were at the transverse road that led across the park at Eighty-sixth Street. She went, knowing that if she stopped, he would do whatever he planned to do at once, without any delay. And, like the moments stolen during the beatings of her mother, she lived from reprieve to reprieve.

"Mickey, I swear!" she cried as they hiked. It was already growing dark.

"Right," he said. His voice was hoarse and his march was steady and they advanced past the park's reservoir to the Great Lawn. In the twilight she could see figures moving quickly in the shadows—people fleeing the park, leaving it to the denizens of the night. The trees were bare and the shrubbery had shed its flowers, but there were still hiding places everywhere.

They stopped in front of a large clump of bare bushes. He stood holding her with his right hand—a grip that she could never break—and grasping something in his left hand.

"I swear," she said in a low, desperate voice. She knew that if she raised her voice, it would trigger a further, more dangerous stage of ferocity.

"I wanna ask you something," he said. His voice had the controlled temper of a trap. "I wanna ask you, how am I gonna live now? I mean, how the fuck am I gonna live? You know what I mean? My brothers, my friends, how am I gonna look at them? You understand what I'm asking you?"

She spoke slowly, deliberately, enunciating and pleading at the same time. "Mickey, I will go to them—each and every one—and tell them exactly what happened."

She could see him shaking his head in the darkening night. "You can't convince me, so how are you gonna convince my brothers? You remember my brothers. They'll think I'm a fag if I don't do something. You know? It's like the Middle Ages when you had to die if you dishonored someone. You dishonored me, Peg. Someone's gotta pay for that."

When he came toward her, he kicked something. It moved. Then it muttered an oath. "Watch where the fuck you're going!"

It was a woman. She had been asleep near the bushes. She had risen to her knees and was struggling to get to her feet. She was whip thin and wrapped in a blanket. A derelict with a plastic black garbage bag full of trash possessions.

Mickey stopped and turned and made a movement that Peggy only recognized in retrospect. He whipped his left hand around and it passed in front of the woman's face. Peggy didn't even notice the contact. She only saw a flap of flesh fall away from the woman's cheek and blood begin to spill out in a great gush. The woman didn't say anything, just gagged. Peggy could see the surprised look on her face.

Then she watched Mickey close in, bend over, and move his hand again; this time it went across the woman's throat, which opened as if he were slicing an orange. She was dead by the time she fell back against the bush that had been her last home.

Mickey stood there, breathing hard. Peggy whimpered.

"Shut the fuck up!" he hissed. She couldn't help it and started to back away, thinking, That could have been me, that was going to be me—I'm looking through a glass at my own bloody murder! "If you don't keep quiet, I'll do you!" he said again in that snake voice.

She lost track of how long they stood there. Then he took a deep breath and came to a decision. He reached down and picked up a rock. It was a heavy rock, more than a foot across, and Peggy thought that he intended to use it on her. But he handed it to her.

"I want you to bash in her brains," he said.

She was startled. It was a trick, she decided. Then she thought briefly of trying to defend herself, using the rock against Mickey. But that would be suicide. He still held the razor-sharp knife in his left hand.

"Hit her!" he ordered.

And she did. It was no big deal, she told herself. The woman was already dead. If it placated him, if it bought her more time, it was a sensible thing to do. What made her ill was what Mickey did afterward. He tore into the body as if he were a surgeon. He stripped the woman bare and took large chunks out of the corpse.

"We're gonna have some fun," he said. "If you're not lying to me about what you said."

"I swear, Mickey!"

"We're gonna have some fun."

THREE

On the evening of her first completely handcrafted dinner party, Detective Lieutenant Maggie Van Zandt cooked her gun. She intended chicken. But old habits die hard.

At 6:20, when she arrived home from the supermarket, with her arms laden with bundles of food, she had little more than an hour to prepare the meal. But there were other things on her mind. In fact, Maggie's attention was scattered, not unlike the unmarked boxes of clothing and household goods lying exactly where the movers had deposited them seven days earlier. Outlines of dust had already formed around the unpacked cartons. Like the chalk markings of a crime scene, she thought.

In addition to the pressure to someday unpack, plus the requirement to prepare and plate some food, she had on her mind a fresh and unmerciful murder—something that outranked all other considerations in her hierarchy of significance. Still, there was nothing she could do about it at the moment. Assignments had been made, investigators were out, steps had been taken. Yet given all that pressure, her concentration snapped and she simply stuffed her .38 caliber service revolver into the oven. It was a habit left over from her old, uptown apartment where the oven had been the ideal deep, safe-storage burial site for the weapon.

Maggie dreaded the thought of a loaded gun floating between rooms. And since, in her old apartment, there was not much chance of her actually using the oven for cooking, that's where she kept it.

But this was the new place—in the Bohemian quarter of Manhattan's Greenwich Village—and on this particular night, for the official installation ceremony, she had promised an old-fashioned home-cooked meal, which called for full oven participation.

And so, after she routinely disposed of the gun, Maggie began emptying the bags of food. When she came across the raw chicken—a shockingly lurid sight for a person who does not normally cook—she sighed, reminded herself that she had only herself to blame, and got down to business. She slapped oil and herbs and garlic on the carcass of the dead chicken as if she were trying to revive it. It took her a moment to remember to reach inside the chicken's cavity and remove the giblets (like birthing a baby, she thought miserably); she then spanked some more oil and herbs and garlic on the rubbery skin.

While her hands were slimy with oil and blood, she thought of something else—lethal salmonella bacteria. Chickens were perfect breeding grounds for deadly germs; that was the disturbing message regularly broadcast by local TV health alarmists. Like most civilians, Maggie was defenseless against TV hysterics. So she interrupted the seasoning operation to scrub down the chicken with hot soapy water, which, according to vague memory, was the approved decontamination method. This was followed by another vigorous application of oils and herbs, which, she noted, were running low. Then she jammed the whole foul mess into a roasting pan and stuffed it inside the oven. She was relieved to get rid of it.

That fleeting instant of unclouded satisfaction was broken by the realization that she was sweating. She was still wearing her topcoat.

After removing it, she spent five minutes fiddling with space-age dials and knobs, activating electric coils, and muttering at her new flameless, high-tech, energy-efficient electric oven. She rolled her eyes and gnashed her unstable teeth, sensing a deep sounding of impending dental woe. A lifelong cavity-prone victim of substandard teeth, Maggie was having a bad dental day (all-too-familiar images of frowning, clucking dentists, together with a fresh influx of hefty bills, came instantly to mind), and so she did not yet notice the gun roasting alongside the chicken.

Fortunately she was a fretful chef and kept opening the glass door of the oven and poking her head inside to make sure that the chicken was reacting properly to the 425-degree temperature. Then, standing back and admiring her handiwork, she observed a thin metal switch near the handle of the door. A light switch. When she flicked it, a bulb illuminated the interior of the appliance. At that instant she was both pleased and horrified. For there, jammed up against the pan containing the chicken in the blistering belly of the beast, she saw her service revolver roasting at high heat. Groaning at her own stupidity, she reached inside and grabbed the weapon by the metal barrel. Which was how she cooked her fingers.

She was not cut out for the domestic arts, she grumbled under her breath; it required a degree of diligence and clear concentration that she did not possess. Then she did what she always did when faced with dense and implacable frustration: She took a shower.

Even under the gust of steamy water, she thought of the body in the park. Technically, as head of the Manhattan North Homicide Command, it was her corpse. The body had been found—like most bodies detected in the park—by a jogger. The dawn patrol of joggers marked the night's carcasses for collection on their rounds like aerobic scouts. Then they stayed there, ran in place to keep their own blood pumping, a grim, pounding congregation of heart-healthy spectators, while the emergency squads and morticians sealed off the area and attended to the imperative terminal transactions.

Maggie had been in her second-floor, glass-encased office at Manhattan North Homicide Command on East Fifty-first Street, having one of those arid, paper-chase mornings, when she read about the dead woman in the reports. She was moving routine items from the In basket to the Out basket; charting attendance of the members of the command, reviewing expense accounts, approving vacations—handling, in short, the accounting end of running a homicide command. And then she came across the body in the park.

She read the wintry details of the killing with her usual professionally controlled sense of indignation. The insults to the victim were punched in on a defective typewriter (letters riding up, down, and sideways across the page) by the heavy-handed first-grade detective who caught the case: *Sex:* Female; *Race:* Caucasian; *Age:* between thirty and forty-five; *Hair:* brown; *Eyes:* none. Under the notes, there was an explanation. The eyes had been gouged out. Also, the fingertips had been cut off, the teeth had been extracted, the face had been mashed to a pulp. The throat had been slit. The corpse was naked. Everything had been obliterated to defeat identification. The catching detective, with that impish cruelty that evolves from a little-boy sadism, had typed on the last line, *Cause of Death:* HOMICIDE.

Yes, well, thought Maggie as she read the report, definitely not a suicide. And not just one more of New York's dozen daily murders. This one had the characteristics of an intense and brutal mystery. It shouldn't have shocked her, given the high level of urban rage that ran through the high-strung city. But the elements—so neatly and indifferently set forth in chilly bureaucratic police vernacular—had an extra, disfiguring element of ruthlessness, and the case stayed with Maggie all day long.

Part of the shock came from the location. Central Park should have been a sanctuary. It was an extravagance, setting aside 843 acres in the heart of Manhattan, where every inch of space was measured and counted like precious diamonds. But forget the cost—the park was a great breath of needed rest from the intense streets. There were in the park vast tracts of trees, long rolling fields, clipped lawns, a tiny zoo, a merry-go-round, and lonely trails.

During the day you could see the nannies trailing children who trailed balloons, and there was a suggestion of pastoral innocence, a nineteenth-century illusion of serenity. Of course that soft fantasy departed quickly at night—fled, like the romantic strollers who raced for the exits. In the dark—as in a nightmare forest—the trees and shrubs became hiding places for maniacs. And in the morning, the cops who fanned out from the Arsenal Precinct, in the center of the transverse, would find the remnants of the predators. The makeshift beds of cardboard boxes, the empty crack vials, the bent needles and pools of blood. Sometimes not even a body, just a pool of unexplained blood. And, often enough, there would be TV crews behind yellow tape, filming crime scenes and interviewing the joggers, who were still jogging in their automatic piston fashion.

The television crews waited politely in line for their turn to stand behind the yellow tape for their exclusively indistinguishable stories. Not that there was much to change. They all recognized the implicit drama of the incongruous backdrop—sylvan trees and unblemished fields, and the body bags and the somber detectives and the flashing lights of the emergency vehicles. The TV reporters all performed their stand-ups about the mutilated woman with the *good visuals* behind them.

Recognizing immediately that this had high-profile possibilities, Maggie went up to the Great Lawn in the park, toured the crime scene, made certain that it was being given a high enough priority, considering all the newsworthy ingredients. Could not be caught deficient by the press, who circled stories like hawks looking for a weakness. She assigned extra detectives, guessing that it would probably turn out to be a psychoderelict thing. One of the homeless queens who lived in the bushes and would turn out to be ten years younger than anyone guessed. Still, an investigative team was brought together. Uniformed patrols organized sweeps of known park dwellers, habitués, voyeurs, and passersby. Doormen at the swank buildings on the fringes of the park were being questioned. A search was being conducted. A tally was being made. The stones were being turned.

And in the first rush of investigation nothing presented itself. It was common police wisdom that if the solution didn't show itself immediately—some blood-caked lover, some enraged junkie, some traces of a gang—it would probably take a while to crack the case. Then it would come as a lucky break somewhere down the road. Someone picked up for something else would trade this solution for a chunk of prison time.

Meanwhile, all she could do was order a check of the missing persons, canvass the neighborhoods, allow the media to ventilate the mystery and maybe produce—after the crackpots exhausted themselves—a lead. A file was opened up. Reports were sent downtown so that the superchiefs could talk knowingly to their reporter cronies. Maggie had done all that was expected, all that a single murder called for. Nevertheless a woman mutilated out of existence still made her shudder. That bad feeling lingered, even when she came home, even when she shopped, and it stayed when she climbed into the hot shower.

Eventually, the water cure worked. When she stepped out of the shower and onto the mat, Maggie's mood was almost serene. She glanced at the mirror and she saw that her stomach was flat, her skin was pink, her features were, as always, a pure surprise. Maggie was fair in a surprisingly effortless, straightforward manner, without tricks or exertion. Hers was an everyday, durable attractiveness. Not that she took any credit for it. Maggie's life was too crowded with substance to bother with vanity, grooming, or intricate fashion strategies. Her hair fell where the brush left it. Her figure lingered where the meals and her all-out pace concluded. She certainly couldn't take pride in the high flush of her skin; it was an outgrowth of her natural energy and enthusiasm. And she was not responsible for her features—a biological remnant of plain genetics.

To the extent that it deflected attention from her intelligence—became the first thing that many men in her male-dominated profession noticed and remarked upon—she resented the fact that she was, after all, a lush, appealing thirty-four-year-old woman. If she had to, she would concede that her good looks gave her some career advantages. In her rise through the police department, superior officers, chauvinist partners, dangerous felons had all been ambushed by the unblinking, sharp, and savage intelligence that lay behind the deceptively artless exterior.

As she stood there in front of the mirror, regarding herself with critical neutrality, Maggie realized that she had no reason for her bad mood. Her job had meaning; she had a decent man in her life; her health was robust, with the exception of her sickly teeth. Nevertheless, apart from the usual inventory of biological, ecological, and sociological disasters that awaited everyone in the twenty-first century, she was relatively happy. Or, as happy and satisfied as a volatile, tempestuous, vaguely cranky, and chronically impatient woman ever could be. If her nature and temperament were not designed for deep and lasting contentment, they were good material for a detective lieutenant in charge of a homicide division.

As for her quirky and contradictory temperament, she ascribed that to a mother with Irish terrorist sympathies and a father who had the stone-stubborn traits of a Dutch merchant. This explained her strange, uneven conduct. One moment she was a stiff-necked cop with no emotions, the next a softhearted patsy dropping a five-dollar bill into the cup of a legless beggar.

As she dried her hair, lazily humming tunes from *Showboat*, she suddenly realized that Jerry would soon be ringing the bell, expecting, of all things, a home-cooked meal. She had half an hour. Why, she cried aloud, did she ever agree to this home-cooked madness?

Well, she knew why. Because it was required. It became clear to her in one of those blazing emotional and intellectual insights that, sooner or later, men and women reach a stage in a courtship when restaurant dinners and takeout food are not enough. They may have slept together, they may have taken trips together and revealed the innermost secrets of their innermost hearts; they may even have sworn deathless oaths and felt rare emotions, but it was still not enough. There was one more solemn ritual betokening true and profound sentiment: She had to feed and water him. It was, of course, a pagan and primitive retro act, but all the same, it had to be done.

Beyond that, the meal had to be handmade. Not some low, takeout version of a sit-down spread. It had to be freshly drawn from the earth, tenderly washed and carefully seasoned and lovingly kneaded and chopped; it had to be cooked by her own hand, served on real china with fresh linen underneath. Finally, grudgingly, mutinously, Maggie arrived at the inescapable conclusion that she had to cook something for Jerry Munk, her man. And the poor bastard had to eat it.

In the past, whenever the topic presented itself—usually after Jerry cooked for her and a reciprocal gesture seemed in order—Maggie wiggled out of it, telling herself that she was technically incapable of preparing a full-fledged dinner. She even had a solid list of very good alibis. First, her old kitchen in the tiny fragment of an apartment on the Upper West Side of Manhattan was too small. And then there was the fact that her appliances were inadequate. The stove was cranky, the space was cramped, the implements didn't fit the room—the stars were all against it.

In fact, as accomplished as she was at most things, as high as she scored on cognitive exams, as brilliant as she was at solving complex criminal riddles, Maggie did not believe that she could pull off a proper meal. Not with appropriate wine and sensible balanced courses and matched dinnerware. And then there was her fail-safe excuse: her job. She was on call—emergency signals could begin to flash for her twenty-four hours a day. What if the beeper went off in the middle of the entrée?

Eventually, as she knew that she would, she ran out of lame excuses and issued the command invitation: Dinner, she announced to the startled companion. I'm cooking!

Aware of every tricky implication, Jerry Munk, the boyfriend, the significant other, the man in the bull's-eye of this culinary longshot, became pale and clammy when he received this summons. "When?" he asked in his irritatingly practical way.

That left Maggie momentarily stumped. Now she had to come up with prosaic details, particulars of when, what, and how. The menu—what could she possibly prepare? There were also the issues of suitable china, matched flatware, unbroken crystal. But above all there was the apartment. Her single room on the Upper West Side of Manhattan was a playpen. A very crowded, very inadequate playpen.

Maggie dealt with that problem. She moved.

She gave up the Upper West Side playpen and found a grown-up apartment in one of those rehab units with a full kitchen and a cooking island, as well as a modern, electric, state-of-the-art stove. It also came with a doorman and a superintendent and a mailbox that locked. She felt—at least for that first week—well groomed.

FOUR

The Gotham on Thirty-first Street off Lexington Avenue was one of those splinter hotels on the fringe of the garment district, tucked between ready-to-wear sweatshops and a Greek coffee shop. If it had seen better days, they weren't much better.

There had been a time when it was used by buyers who came to town to do business and wanted nothing more than a bed and a roof before they made a quick exit back to the Midwest. But the rag trade wasn't like that anymore. The out-of-town buyers didn't need to test the merchandise; they bought wholesale from catalogues or discount chains or massive factory outlets, and if they came to New York, they stayed at the Hilton or some other high-priced Midtown chain where they could get room service and a reasonably priced hooker.

Over the years, the Gotham had turned into the equivalent of a residency harlot. It was now a single room occupancy hotel, pinching out whatever the traffic would bear from a cross section of minimum-wage waiters, recovering substance abusers, part-time clerks—all the shadowy denizens of the city who lived in the cracks between a substantial world of home, job, and family and the rootless derelicts who lived in doorways. For a few hundred dollars a month, the transient trade got an airless room that overlooked an alley, a bed that sagged, a dresser plucked from a garbage heap—and the beauty of silent acceptance. No questions were asked at the Gotham.

The desk clerk at the Gotham Hotel was named Lenny, and he was small and thin and was of an uncertain age. He had a rodentlike, watchful alacrity. From behind his bulletproof window, he watched Peggy O'Neill walk quickly past him, her arms loaded down with packages of fast food and some newspapers. She went up the stairs to her third-floor room. She could have used the elevator, but the guests at the Gotham all had their secret quirks.

He made a little mark on a card and would add a twenty-five-dollar charge for the forbidden act of bringing food to the room. Nothing with any mercenary possibilities passed Lenny's eyes.

Fighting the broken lock, Peggy stumbled into room 315. Mickey was sitting on the bed where she had left him, smoldering at a whole new set of swollen grievances—the music down the hall was too loud, the window leaked cold air, his ex-wife had taken too long or had gotten the wrong things on her errands. He grabbed the hamburgers and french fries and the beer out of her hands.

"Where's the change?"

She handed him a few singles and some silver, which he stuffed into his pants pocket, and he began jamming food and beer into his mouth. Before they checked in, Peggy had emptied out her entire bank balance from an automatic teller machine. Mickey had taken charge of the $727. Fifty had gone as a bribe to the clerk to give them a room when he said that they were all full up. Another $175 had gone for two weeks rent on the room. After cabs and incidentals, he had $468 left in his pocket.

He grabbed the newspapers out of her hand and began to leaf through them, looking for something specific. He flung them away on the floor when he was done.

Peggy sat on the broken lounger and picked at her hamburger. She knew that she was his prisoner now. He told her so, and the chains were of her own making. She had used the rock on the woman in the park. She was as guilty of murder as he was. They were in it together.

It was true. She had gone out on her own to run the errands. She had a chance to call a cop, but she didn't. Because she had maybe killed that woman in the park. She was a murderer.

"Here!" he cried, through the mush of food.

He was folding the newspaper over—the *Daily News*—and was showing her an item on an inside page. It read:

> *An apparently homeless woman was found brutally murdered in Central Park early today. Police said that the woman, who was probably in her late 30s or early 40s, had been mutilated by a sadistic killer. There were no further details.*

She gasped. The black-and-white printed proof of what they had done made her dizzy. "Oh, lord!" she cried. "Oh, sweet mother of God, please forgive me!"

Mickey was watching her. Smiling. "Listen, I got an idea," he said. "This will make you feel better. And it will put some hex on those fucks at the TV station."

He told her his plan and she was amazed. She agreed with him—it would alter things. She was not thinking clearly enough to see exactly how it would change what they had done to the homeless woman, but it would shock the people at the TV show.

She left him there, eating the remains of her hamburger, while she went out to do what he told her to do.

Patrolman Pudge Keene, on anticrime sentry duty at the northeast corner of Fifth Avenue and Fifty-ninth Street near F.A.O. Schwarz, heard a cry for help coming out of his belly. It was hunger. Pudge Keene quit searching for pickpockets and purse snatchers and concentrated instead on finding his partner, Freddie "the Man" Murphy, who had gone for sandwiches. It was a few minutes after seven in the evening and Patrolman Pudge Keene was not accustomed to eating so late.

In spite of being called Pudge, there was not much fat on

Jimmy Keene's lanky frame. He was awarded the nickname in recognition of his great appetite (a man who could put away three supersubs at a sitting surely would one day eat his way into that heavier classification). It was also a clear demonstration of mean-spirited cop humor—if the boys in the Anticrime Task Force sensed a weakness, they would rub it raw.

He didn't mind. Pudge was a good sport, happy to be a cop, easy with the locker-room jibes of his colleagues. If, at the moment, he felt odd, uneasy, and out of place, it was because he was working undercover in the most glamorous section of the city, the area around the glittering southeastern crown of Central Park. It was a golden realm of the city, ablush with fancy hotels and swanky shops and expensive restaurants. Pudge was dazzled by the swirl of celebrities, socialites, and power brokers, along with the softer, statelier flow of old-money aristocrats. He was moved just by the sight of them gliding into stretch limousines as smoothly as if they were slipping on a pair of long silk gloves.

Embarrassed by the sounds coming out of his stomach, Pudge looked east, toward Madison Avenue, where, by now, Patrolman Freddie "the Man" Murphy should have been heading back. Pudge and the Man were partnered up on pickpocket patrol in the Midtown Anticrime Task Force—an assignment intended to slow down street crime in the heart of Manhattan's lush East Side.

Pudge took his undercover role seriously and tried to appear like any other cocky construction worker, lingering on his break with the blue-collar contempt for the idle rich and leering at any passing female. He drew the line at making animal noises. He wore a bulky bubble jacket, an exhausted knit cap, and a pair of patched woolen gloves, and he tried with a pressed brow to communicate attitude. All he managed to convey was a look of anguish. High up on the items bothering Pudge was a technical flaw in his disguise. He kept his service revolver in an ankle holster, and he worried that in an emergency he'd be unable to get at it quickly enough.

His partner had no such concerns. The Man Murph kept his weapon brazenly apparent in a shoulder holster—wanted it known, displayed it as a kind of visual deterrent. He ridiculed Pudge's efforts at disguise. At twenty-four, the Man Murph was a year younger than Pudge Keene, but he came out of the ghetto and thus got credit for postgraduate street wisdom; being Black aged a man, he said, made him years older when it came to the tricky ways of the city. The Man didn't even try to look "undercover"; he wore his finest gold rings and chains, his newest hightops, a creamy leather jacket, and a white scarf, and he walked with a robust and defiant swagger. The only thing that the Man worried about was not looking cool.

"You think we're foolin' somebody?" he would ask Pudge in the tone of a college dean delivering remedial instruction to a slow learner. "You think they see a White guy and a Black guy hanging out together and they think, 'Oh, yeah, there's a couple of homeys about to cut loose'? What the fuck's wrong with you? A White guy and a Black guy? The picks, man, they know who the fuck we are! They track us, like enemy radar. They factor us into the criminal equation! Like counting lampposts and getaway routes and rush-hour jams. They make us for fuckin' heat from the git-go! We ain't foolin' nobody."

"So why don't they wait till we're gone?" Pudge would ask in an attitude of infuriatingly obtuse reason.

"Man, you are so dumb it's pathetic, you know that? The reason they don't wait till we're gone—you listenin' to me?—is for the fuckin' game, man. It's a challenge. The fuck-it game! The beat-the-fuckin'-man game. The we-are-fuckin'-with-your-sister game. You see what I'm sayin'? Why do they jump a turnstile when it just takes some coin to go clean? Do you understand what I'm trying to tell you? Oh, man, why do they always stick me with the lip-readers?"

Pudge understood the point, but he didn't agree. He grew up along the blue-collar spine of Queens, an outer borough thick with unyielding ignorance and hardened racist assumptions. The retired cops and firemen on Northern Boulevard simply did not give Black people credit for clear thinking. And they never ascribed their own brittle convictions to prejudice—just blunt candor.

As a child of that contaminated soil, Pudge thought, in his mild ignorance, that since he and the Man Murph were partners, they were therefore friends.

Although the Man knew better, he nevertheless enjoyed Pudge's company. He recognized the imprint of Pudge's bigoted root, but he could not get past the fact that his partner was likable and so he granted him conditional absolution. When the Man was driven to the edge of frustration by Pudge's careless racism, he settled for a small outpouring of steam: "You could be buck naked and the picks would know who the fuck you are, you know that? You got that ofay Long Island dumb look!"

After tonight's lecture, it was the Man Murph's turn to get the sandwiches, a rotation that the Man told Pudge, in his sly, manipulative manner, always made him feel bad. Disrespected, he said movingly. After all, superior street wisdom should entitle him to some seniority advantages. Add to that the psychological hardship that "fetching" dinner posed for a Black man; it conjured up negative slave images.

There were times when Pudge—feeling vaguely guilty and having at bottom a streak of pure decency—went for the food in spite of the fact that he kept strict accounts when it came to fair play. Just to avoid a fuss. But tonight, Pudge kept silent, didn't volunteer, and let the Man go for the dinner.

Pudge hoped that he wouldn't have to pay for it. When the Man Murph went for the sandwiches he always forgot the pickle, and Pudge was starting to think maybe it was no accident. Some little payback thing.

That's what he was thinking when he noticed a tall shabby man—layers and layers of coats and scarves and fabric—bending and searching through a trash can across Fifty-ninth Street. The derelict looked like a living heap of filthy laundry, diving into the refuse container on the southeast corner. Looking for deposit cans, thought Pudge dismissively. Tough night to be fishing for nickle-deposit soda cans. There were street vendors out in the cold, but they didn't sell too many cold drinks in midwinter. In January tourists and shoppers wanted hot pretzels and chestnuts.

Then Pudge saw a second hand reach out from another crevice in the mound of clothing and plunge into the garbage to pluck something out. It was a woman's purse. A large purse. Not one of the fancy useless things from Bergdorf Goodman just big enough for a little lipstick. The two hands held up the purse to the light, and the man looked at it through the tunnel opening that had been fashioned as a hood. Pudge strained to see, too. Utilitarian, he thought of the bag. Someone could fit a change of shoes, along with gloves and a scarf and a sweater, as well as a wallet, into that thing. Definitely a working purse. The hands holding the purse now retreated along with the bag toward the deep bowels of the textile refuge.

"Hey!" Pudge yelled, charging across the street, holding up a hand against the honking traffic, thinking that once the purse got inside that pile of rags, he'd never be able to find it again.

The hood swiveled in Pudge's direction like a periscope, paused for a second to confirm the recognition, then the entire pile of rags began to move away, both hands grasping the purse. It was not so unusual to see a moving stack of old clothes in Midtown, where men crawled out of flattened cardboard houses and the homeless lived in bags and boxes. There were makeshift shelters inside every dark doorway and over every steam vent. The unfortunate urban homeless were, for the most part, pathetic creatures—slow-moving, cringing, and only latently ominous. But when the tall mound of clothing ran east on Fifty-ninth Street and started to pick up speed at an alarming rate, it forced panicky gaps in the normally unruffled pedestrian traffic. The natives moved with veteran grace, sidestepping the approaching heap like tango dancers, eyelids only slightly raised at the swift approach of the odd, potentially dangerous pile of clothing.

Pudge had to fight his way through, since the tide closed in behind the escaping rags; the pedestrians were curious, albeit in that deadened, hard-to-budge, Manhattan spectator fashion.

Pudge couldn't decide whether to go for his weapon or wait until he got closer; he was running and hopping, staggering with indecision. He clawed at his coat collar to free the leather necklace that held his silver shield. "Police!" he cried, causing less interest and much less response than the man running under the great burden of textiles. "Police! Halt!"

The guy was fast, he thought, as he lost ground trying not to knock people over, feeling the cold sweat of action.

And then he saw the handbag fly up into the air, launched along with a brown paper bag full of wrapped sandwiches, by a collision. When he pushed his way through the circle of spectators he saw the Man on top of the pile of rags, slapping cuffs on one hand of the fallen derelict.

"Where's the victim?" he asked Pudge, searching for the second hand in the complicated folds of the derelict's garments.

From inside the hood came soft cries of protest, smothered by all the apparel.

The rookie cop was confused.

"Where's the damn victim?" repeated the Man.

"I think he took the bag out of a garbage can," stammered Pudge. "I didn't see a victim."

The Man had found the derelict's second hand and lashed it to the first. He kept his knee on the derelict's back, holding him down, while radioing in for backup and transport. Pudge noticed that he already had his shield out—how did he get it out so quick? he wondered. But the Man was always careful about showing himself as a cop. "Black man with a gun in Midtown is in big trouble unless he is in uniform, and even then . . .," he had often told Pudge.

"He took the bag out of a garbarge can. I saw him do it. Should I go look for the victim?"

The Man shook his head, fully alert, his weapon still holstered. "Stay with your partner," he said acidly. Another reproach.

When they got back to Manhattan North on East Fifty-first Street, Pudge and the Man marched the dazed derelict upstairs to be questioned by the detectives. The homeless man kept muttering that he found the purse in the garbage, that he had committed no crime. But he was homeless and smelly and Black and had possession of someone else's property. No one paid any attention until the female cop on computer property inventory duty went through the purse. She found an informal ID card—the kind that comes with a wallet. The name on the card was Peggy O'Neill.

FIVE

After the shower, Maggie found herself in the bedroom, staring at a drawer bubbling with excess paper. When she pulled on the handle of the drawer, an autumn of unpaid bills came floating out, drifting gracefully down to the carpet in gentle, swooning circles. They had the range of burnt colors of fallen leaves—pink and red and amber. Overdue notices. She stared at the bills and remembered putting them away—one or two at a time—but not so many. How had they accumulated so quickly?

Well, she had spent a few weeks in Paris and Florence chasing a phantom killer; things had inevitably piled up. On top of that there was the turmoil of the move. Packing. Almost unpacking. Thinking about the dinner.

In fact, she hated paying credit-card bills. Before she took them seriously, they had to ripen from pale perfumed reminders into pungent pink warnings, then burst out of her mailbox as flaming red threats.

From time to time she gave herself a talk, reminded herself that a lieutenant of detectives had an obligation to set high moral and ethical standards. On the other hand, she eventually paid the bills. She always paid the bills. But she had that granular tendency to march up to the edge of default before dropping the check in the mail.

It was not a matter of bad character. She just didn't like being pushed—that nugget of Irish and Dutch pride. And then there was the appeal of chaos. Maggie was one of those rare people who are comfortable amid the clamor and clutter of bedlam. It tended to focus her concentration on matters of real importance—like catching felons and murderers.

That was her specialty. If she slipped into untidy checkbook habits, she told herself that it was the triage of her trade. Overdue subscription notices did not rise to the more critical obligation of catching a killer.

While musing about the bills and the theory of social relativity, Maggie smelled the chicken burning. She scampered out of the bedroom, smearing cream on her burned fingers, then scraped the black crust off the surface of the chicken. She dressed quickly, wearing her shoulder holster under her suit jacket to keep track of her gun now that the oven was unsafe. And she began to assemble the dinner.

Since she had forgotten to pick up onions or tomatoes or cucumbers, the salad would be plain lettuce. Minimalist. Very chic. The dressing would be bottled, but she decanted it into a gravy bowl. The pasta would be her own, although the sauce came out of a jar. The blistered chicken was definitely hers. Then she noticed that she did not have wine. Fifteen minutes. There was time.

Stepping out into the cold night, she inhaled the fresh, crisp, piney air of her new neighborhood. It was one of those uncommon evenings when Sheridan Square had an intoxicating, nineteenth-century coal and chimney hue; the streets were crowded with its usual whimsical Bohemians—caped artists and whiskered writers and windblown poets. There was a young, festive feel in the Village—as if the holidays had just begun. People coming from work were in a jaunty, almost friendly mood. Shops were busy and full of lighthearted energy. The citizens were polite—for New Yorkers. They still bumped into each other (New Yorkers insisted on their egalitarian right to bump each other). But there was a noticeable softening of the ensuing glares. Instead of duking it out, they just kept walking at their normal getaway pace. Maggie felt a tender winter tang as she hurried along Seventh Avenue searching for a liquor store.

She found one near Christopher Street and bought two bottles of expensive red cabernet sauvignon and filled out an application for a store charge account. The owner rang up the wine on the charge—an act of faith—and she felt an unaccustomed coziness and acceptance. It augured well. A housewarming gift of approval from the community.

Jerry Munk was waiting for her when she got back to her apartment building. "Sorry," she said, but it wasn't necessary. They both brightened when they saw each other. They had been dating for seven months (if a woman in her midthirties and a man who was tiptoing over the edge of forty can be designated as "dates"), and still experienced a burst of unexpected delight when they saw each other. Every encounter was a shock. It was very disturbing to Maggie.

It was also upsetting to Jerry Munk, who had hardened himself against someone like Maggie invading his life. He was a former newspaperman and he had an automatic aversion to cops. And yet Jerry Munk allowed Maggie to crack that resistance. It was the odd, mutinous side of her nature that changed his mind. And there were ancient, unspoken understandings. They chatted in half sentences, nodding and grinning like idiots.

Maggie heard an echo in Jerry's insubordinate credo. Jerry Munk had quit a golden newspaper job over a matter of principle. Principle, along with a recognition that he had outlived certain frames of reference and was thus rendered intellectually obsolete. He was beginning to meet educated young reporters who could not remember *The Front Page* or who had never read Upton Sinclair or were unfamiliar with the angry spirit of wild rebellion that propelled him into the newspaper business in the first place.

He had joined the profession to be among the untamed editors who ran every story to the edge of sedition. Their common aim was to break the authority of anyone in charge of anything.

But journalism changed sometime after Watergate. The fearless editors had mutated into corporate shopkeepers. They wore fancy suspenders and presided solemnly over meetings about trends and celebrity gossip. The happy breed was gone.

And so Jerry Munk quit and opened a bookstore on the Upper West Side of Manhattan where he could withdraw into the clarity and comfort of Henry James and Thoreau and Edmund Wilson. He was astonished that it took a cop to drag him back into the late twentieth century. He felt as if he had been placed under emotional arrest.

They rode up the elevator chattering over one another's conversation comfortably, him saying that they could still eat out, he didn't mind, her shaking her head and cataloguing and enumerating the endless preparations and care that good cooking required. The washing, the dicing, the split-second timing! It was a goddamned art! Tonight, she was a kitchen Michelangelo.

"You know, the everyday details of life are really fulfilling," she said, unlocking the front door of her apartment. Jerry didn't know what to make of this odd, half-housebroken Maggie and agreed in a vague, nodding sort of way. Then, as Maggie pushed open the door, he saw the untouched cartons in the same rough state as the day she moved in, and he burst out laughing.

"Clean off a spot on the couch," she said sideways, with the sham impatience of a spouse.

He was pleased and amused and obedient and arranged the table while Maggie was in the kitchen dishing out the meal.

"This is delicious," said Jerry Munk, trying to swallow a large chunk of scorched chicken.

"Maybe we should try the pasta," suggested Maggie, who was ready to start on the second bottle of wine.

"I like the chicken," said Jerry.

"Try the damn pasta," said Maggie.

Just then they heard the buzz of her beeper. An emergency.

"Saved by the bell," said Jerry, putting the last piece of chicken from his mouth into his napkin.

SIX

The calls began with the first hint of a solid link between the mutilated body in the park and the missing guest on the TV talk show. A low-level precinct detective at the One Seven phoned a legman on a tabloid newspaper and tipped him off that a juicy story involving big-shot celebrities and a gory homicide was about to break. You couldn't keep such a thing secret. Every live cop had a private dream of a seven-figure book contract.

After that first call, the dam broke. The tabloid legman called a friend downtown in the public-relations office of police headquarters for confirmation. The friend in the Public Affairs Department called Marty Klein, the deputy commissioner for public affairs, who called the chief of detectives, who alerted the police commissioner, who summoned the mayor out of a fund-raising dinner at the Waldorf-Astoria.

And the mayor, who was married to a former TV reporter, told his wife, who—because she once interviewed him and thus regarded him as an intimate friend—called Kevin Grant and alerted him to batten down for an approaching media gale.

By the time Maggie Van Zandt walked into the headquarters of Manhattan North Homicide on East Fifty-first Street, the atmosphere was thick with impending crisis. Not the functional cop trouble of a wild shootout or a hot chase. This was the silent, sullen disquiet of second-guessing politicians and oppressive, sharpshooting superior officers who were going to pick apart every step of the investigation. This was high-profile news. Instead of the sunny banter of shifts going out on patrol, she heard a gloomy hush.

The desk sergeant was one of those grizzled old-timers who had made enough laps around the streets of the city to loaf through his last tour of duty. Now he stood behind the high magistrate's perch, observing his world with a sour glare.

"Somebody nail the mayor's wife for illegal parking?" Maggie asked brightly, signing the log.

The desk sergeant gave Maggie a small, bitter smile and rolled his eyes upstairs to her base, the headquarters of the Manhattan North Homicide Command. Like all good cops, the desk sergeant didn't like unexpected high police officials showing up on his territory. She nodded, having seen the name of Chief of Detectives Larry Scott on the sign-in sheet.

She hurried up the stairs and found a few of her detectives gathering—sleepy from the trip in from the suburbs, crabby at being roused from their TV bunkers or pulled away from the start of a midnight drunk—grudgingly building up a flutter of activity.

Standing near the head of the stairs was Maggie's sidekick, Detective Sergeant Sad Sam Rosen, holding a stack of reports. He looked bone weary and deeply worried. It was his standard condition. The fact that he was Black, as well as a Jew, along with the added tricky ingredient of being a cop, endowed him with a complicated nature—enigmatic and habitually fretful. It was Sam's greathearted quality of withholding judgment that Maggie prized. She used his slow misgivings to adjust and revise her own quick tendencies.

"You wanna see him first?" he asked, tossing his head back to indicate the office where the chief of detectives was waiting.

"Not yet," she replied.

He handed her the first reports. "He's pissed."

"What's new?"

Sam shrugged. "He asked where the hell you were, then lit up the phones and sent out for coffee and egg sandwiches. He's in there scoffing up caffeine and cholesterol and sucking on dry cigarettes and looking for a scapegoat."

"I get the picture. Okay. Tell me what's going on," she said, holding up the reports, forcing her way through the plainclothes traffic, finding a remote desk behind a thick column so that she could be briefed in private; she had learned early in her career that it was a bad idea to go up against a pissed-off chief of detectives ignorant of the terrain.

"Got a homeless guy who picked a purse out of a garbage can near the park," said Sad Sam economically.

Maggie lifted herself so that she sat on the desk, holding the reports. She knew Sam well enough to let him tell the story. Pushing would only slow him down.

"Woman's purse," he said. "ID inside had the name of Peggy O'Neill."

"Right," she said nodding. "The talk-show woman. So? Is there a link? Is that butchered woman related in some way to Peggy O'Neill?"

He shrugged. "Could be. The purse is a definite. The body in the park is a whole other question. They're making big leaps of intricate assumptions here."

"Well, the possibility is intriguing. If it is the lady from the talk show, there's gonna be a long line to find someone to blame."

"Guess who's at the end of the line."

She nodded. "They're gonna say we should have been looking harder for Peggy O'Neill. Well, because the purse was found near the murder site doesn't mean that we found Peggy."

Sam put up his arms in a gesture of befuddlement. "Listen, it may be totally unrelated. She wasn't reported missing. When she left the office with her ex-husband, there was no hint of trouble.

For all we knew, they coulda been going on a second honeymoon."

"Yeah, I've heard of those honeymoons." She was flipping pages, looking around. "So, who's on our ass?"

"Well, the mayor called the PC, the PC called the chief, and the chief called me and I called you."

She whistled. "A plummeting food chain!" She looked down in thought, read a few more reports. Then, after a moment, she looked up.

"But we have to make certain about this. If the lady in the park is Peggy O'Neill . . ." She didn't finish, just shook her head, which took in a lot of territory. "You're bringing in the guy she worked for, the lawyer. Carr," she ordered.

"He's on his way."

"Put him on ice. Stick him in one of the interrogation rooms till I get to him."

Sad Sam was fifteen years older than Maggie, and that gave him chronological seniority. But she was bright and decisive and could grasp a situation with speed, and that gave her a professional advantage. Together they made a fine team.

"Uh-huh, uh-huh," she said, speaking to the reports. Then, to Sam: "The homeless guy, he turned in the purse? Just a good citizen doing his duty?"

Sam shook his head. "Couple of anticrime kids collared him. Saw him pull it out of the trash can." He shrugged. "Everybody's got to make a living. Then he was dumb enough to make a run for it."

Maggie's face tightened. "Listen, Sam, we didn't happily stumble onto a psychokiller maniac, did we?"

Sam paused, then shook his head. Then, "You should talk to him. He's a character." He shrugged. Sam had a soft spot for unorthodox behavior. Shook his head. "Just a character."

She brought up another report—the incident summary, which gave the police jargon version about the arrest of the homeless man—and waved it at Sam. "This is very thin, Sam. Guy picks a purse out of a garbage can, anybody could do that. That's zilch. Probably just his unlucky day. We don't even know about the body. Maybe it's the talk-show lady, maybe not. How do we get an ID? Forensics will take time. DNA takes weeks."

"I don't even trust DNA . . ."

"And this derelict? I mean, where's the history? What the hell is he, anyway?"

"Just a little homeless."

"No record."

"Not so far."

"Where is he?"

Sam nodded toward the rear. "Interrogation room one."

She got up and marched down the corridor. "Where are the anticrime guys?"

"With him."

They were arranged in blocking positions—Pudge Keene on the left and the Man Murphy on the right—close enough to stop a break for the door. The homeless man had removed his many layers of clothing, including the hooded top, and was sipping coffee and eating a cheese sandwich; he took large bites— an old homeless habit in case someone grabbed the food out of his hands. The garments that he had been wearing were lying in a heap in the corner, removed and searched and left there. He was dressed in a plain sweatshirt and sweatpants and long cotton socks. The sweats were in good condition, picked up at a shelter, donated by tax-shaving Manhattan philanthropists.

The homeless man was Black, early thirties, softly handsome, with a close beard. Cleaned up, coulda been a postgrad student, she thought when she came into the room. He turned and looked up sharply. Alert, she thought, not fogged up with dope or cheap wine. No telling what sorry tale brought him to root through garbage cans for a living.

She put Sam outside the door to await the lawyer, Carr, then took her place behind the single metal desk. The room was dirty and dark, except for the shafts of bright light that came down from the ceiling like bars. There were a few plain chairs and no windows in the room. It was a brutal room. Maggie's gold detective lieutenant's shield was hung around her neck and a blue-and-white ID card was pinned to her jacket. She looked down at the report, then looked up and addressed the homeless man.

"Mr. Benjamin . . ."

He nodded.

"I am Lieutenant Van Zandt."

Before he could say anything, she turned to the Man Murphy. "I assume, Officer, that you have given this man his rights."

"Yes, Lieutenant."

She smiled back at the homeless man. "Technical stuff," she said.

"May be technical to you, lady, but it's my rights," he replied.

When Maggie laughed, everyone in the room joined in.

"You want a lawyer?" she asked.

"Do I need a lawyer?"

"Not unless you did something bad."

He frowned and thought a bit. Then, "Nah. Dropped out of college. Lost my job. Went belly up. That's not against the law."

She nodded, thought: very bright, educated.

She said, "How'd you get to be homeless?"

"You really wanna know? It's a pretty tragic story."

"I can handle it."

"Well, things really went downhill when I took a bold position on AT&T . . ."

They all laughed again. Maggie got up and started to leave. Then she said to the two plainclothes officers, "You can talk to him, but don't question him. Mr. Benjamin is being very cooperative."

In the corridor, Maggie stopped.

"This guy's funny." She shook her head. "We do have the best homeless guys."

"A world-class derelict."

Then Maggie saw a civilian lumbering up the stairs with a pair of accompanying detectives, Matty Bannion and Joey Queen. "Carr?" she asked Sam.

"Probably. I sent Bannion and Queen to bring him in."

She gestured wordlessly, and the detectives and the civilian followed her into the second interrogation room. She took her seat of authority, made certain that everyone had settled down, and folded her hands on the desk.

"You know what this is about, Mr. Carr?"

Maggie's voice had the stone kick of complete authority. It was not unfriendly, but it carried power. Mel Carr looked around and saw that Maggie was talking to him. He was sweating from the stairs and from nerves. Maggie recognized a moment of vulnerability—fear, disorientation. More than one surprise confession was blurted out in this atmosphere. Not that she suspected anything, but it was always better to let the subject of any kind of interrogation walk the plank of information alone.

"I, uh, guess so."

"Peggy O'Neill."

"Yes. Peggy. Have you found her?"

Maggie waited. There was something suggestive about the word *found*. After a sufficient pause, Maggie continued. "You mean, has she turned up?"

"Yes," he replied quickly. "That's what I meant. I mean, why else would you bring me down here in the middle of the night?"

"Why do you think?"

He looked around again. "That bastard, Mickey."

Maggie nodded. She had taken the measure of this one. He was soft and frightened. Not the guilty fear of a killer. The accumulated guilty cuts of a thousand misdemeanors.

"Look, we have a body," she said flatly, watching him stiffen, unable to speak.

Finally, he found his voice. "Peggy?"

"We don't know. We need someone to tell us."

He hung his head.

"May not be easy," Maggie continued. "See, all we have is a body."

He looked up, not comprehending.

"Our body has no face," said Maggie. "Someone turned it into mush." As she spoke, Mel Carr's dinner erupted out of his mouth. Maggie dove to her right, as if she were ducking fire. Detective Matty Bannion tried to grab the wastebasket and jam it under Carr's face, but he only managed to get splattered with the second course of the lawyer's dinner.

"Damn!" shouted Maggie, who escaped the deluge.

"Shit, shit, shit!" shouted Bannion.

Detective Joey Queen laughed.

Sam went for wet paper towels.

"Sorry, sorry, sorry," whimpered Carr, wiping his wet forehead with a handkerchief.

Maggie stood out of range, and asked, "Can you handle this?"

"Yes, yes," said Carr, dipping his handkerchief in a bowl of water brought in by Sam. "It was just the shock."

Outside the office, inside of which Carr and the accompanying detectives were laying a carpet of wet paper towels over the mess, Maggie issued her instructions to Sam.

"See that he gets down to the morgue. I don't think he can make an ID—I saw the body—but you never know. Maybe he knows some unique anatomical detail about Peggy O'Neill. What's left of her anatomy. Keep a bucket and some towels close."

"I'll handle it."

She looked back at interrogation room one, where the homeless man waited. "He's not the type."

"No."

She looked up at the high cobwebbed ceiling. "Still, we better check him out. Run him through all the computers. I'm sure you'll come up blank, but go talk to people at the shelters, bring in an alibi. Something. Get blood, hair, and prints, if he agrees. By the way, did you put an ME on call?"

"Not yet."

"Call one. I want someone down there with Carr. Better yet, call the medical examiner himself. I don't want an assistant. Get him out of bed. This is an all-out O.J. thing if it is the talk-show lady. We don't wanna be caught dumb."

"No."

She looked down the hall at her office, where the chief of detectives waited. "So I guess I gotta talk to Scott."

Sam shrugged. It was a nice eloquent shrug. It contained patient wisdom.

Maggie sighed and issued her orders. "I want some more shoes out on the street. Do it thoroughly, Sam."

"We already have three teams on the case," he said.

"Not enough," explained Maggie. "If it is the talk-show lady that's definitely not enough. Three teams is a gypsy-cab murder. This is a high-profile television killing. TV agents are already optioning the rights. Or, they will be when they hear about it. Six detectives does not sound serious in the newspapers. You need a hefty, round number."

Sam nodded.

She pulled the phone number out of her small pocket address book. It was Deputy Chief Marty Klein's cellular phone. She knew that she couldn't stop the inevitable avalanche of media, but she might be able to slow it down. "Marty, it's Lieutenant Van Zandt."

He didn't seem surprised. "You got a killer yet?"

"I was hoping you had one."

Marty was amused. They spoke the same high style of sarcasm. "Don't call me until you got a killer," said Marty. "I don't deal in concepts or suspects. I'm only here for a solution."

"Listen, Marty, do me a favor; whatever you heard, keep it under your hat for the time being."

"Let me just ask: Have we got a definite connection to the talk-show lady?"

"We don't know, Marty. If it is, you'll be the third person that I notify. Swear."

"Maggie, you are dreaming. I guarantee, there are fifteen reporters and twelve photographers and four TV camera crews on your doorstep at this very minute. That's why I'm avoiding you."

"Okay, Marty, I'm gonna tell them that we have a five-borough task force on this."

"Great," he said. "That's terrific. What's a five-borough task force?"

"Technically, it's called bullshit."

He laughed.

As she entered her own office, where Chief Scott was waiting, she knew that Marty Klein was already calling select and reliable members of the press, giving deep background in exchange for whatever tactical advantage he could negotiate. She had also staked out her territory, made known that she was on top of the case, cleared herself when she made statements to the press. For the later investigation by the sharpshooters.

"Well, Chief," she said, closing the door to her office behind her, "what brings you here?"

Chief Scott was pacing, running out of patience, an unlit cigarette twisting in his hand. He waved the hand, addressing his aide, Sergeant Gil Player. "Wait outside."

When they were alone, Larry Scott spoke softly. It was his way of demonstrating controlled anger. "You got a big case on your hands, Lieutenant."

"Have you been briefed yet, Chief?"

Maggie handled Chief Scott by matching his composure. She walked slowly around the desk, took her seat, and laid the reports in front of her.

As she laid out the facts, Chief Scott looked for an opening. He never wanted a female to head the Manhattan North Homicide Command. He hated the idea. You couldn't talk about down and dirty cop stuff with someone who had to be a presumptive feminist. Always had to be worrying about offending, or not being sensitive. There was something healthy and productive about sitting around all night with the boys—being able to fart, for Christ's sake!—and chewing over the facts of a bigtime murder case.

But the thing that he hated most about Maggie Van Zandt was the fact that he was attracted to her, was moved by her lush beauty, while she had an obstinate immunity to his charms.

When Maggie was done with her presentation, the chief nodded. "Okay. I want Kevin Grant distanced—as much as possible."

"How'm I gonna do that?"

"Kevin Grant is a personal friend of the mayor's wife."

"Listen, boss, I'm running a homicide command. What happens if Kevin Grant's name comes up?"

"Call me."

"Okay, boss. Hey!" She held her hand as if it were a telephone receiver. "Boss? Guess what? The lady in the park might be the guest on *The Kevin Grant Show* and I'm gonna interview him."

He stared at her through eyes narrowed to gun slits. He was trying to decide whether she had crossed the threshold of insubordination.

"Can you talk to him discreetly? Without the media?" he asked meekly.

"Boss, he is the media!"

SEVEN

"Look! Look! C'mere! I wanchata look at this!"

Mickey was sitting up in the bed pointing to the snowy screen of the television set that was bolted to the wall. He was excited, moving up and down. Abruptly, he turned away from the television set for an instant, stopping in midcry to ask, "Didja get the stuff?" When he saw Peggy's quick nod of assent, he swiveled back to the set, eased.

Seeing his relief and feeling a great new surge of power, Peggy closed the door behind her, moved silently into the room, and took a seat.

"You're not gonna believe this! They did a thing, you know, advertising the news, and we was on!"

"It's called a promo," she said quietly.

He turned and she saw the sulphuric look. His face then went through a rainbow of moods—fury, reconsideration, composure. She knew that whole fluctuating range of looks and she was unmoved. After all, she had the stuff. He depended upon her, now that she knew how far things had gone.

Mickey turned up the volume.

"This is Joan Arkin, WCBS News. I am here at the Seventeenth Precinct, Tony, where they are investigating the brutal murder of a woman in Central Park. There are a lot of murders in New York, Tony, but this one has a twist. For one thing the victim was savagely mutilated. According to one detective, it was as if the killer was trying to disguise her identity. The other odd thing about this homicide is that there are indications—and so far they are only indications—that the victim may have been a guest on *The Kevin Grant Show* earlier this week."

Peggy stood up. She saw in her mind a replay of Tuesday's show. She was there. It was her face, her bent posture sitting there on the stage. She remembered now—watching as a spectator— the deep humiliation as she pushed and pushed, trying to please the unpleasable host. She remembered seeing his eyes glaze over with indifference; then he turned away to another guest, dismissing her, dismissing all the years of grief and pain and suffering. All those years and all that heartache wouldn't fit into one short segment of the show. The flashback confirmed for her all the sinister and convoluted conclusions about her plight.

Her attention came back to the TV screen. "This is Lieutenant Margaret Van Zandt, head of the Manhattan North Homicide Command," said the reporter, smiling into the camera.

Maggie Van Zandt had a pained look on her face; it was clear that she was caught between trying to get away from the reporter and the flypaper demands of a live television camera.

"What can you tell us about this case, Lieutenant?" asked the perky reporter.

Mickey and Peggy both closed in on the television set. All respiration in the room had stopped. Only the whistle of the steam heat and the voices from the television could be heard.

"I'm afraid I can't make any comment at this time, Joan," said Maggie pleasantly, then ducked into an unmarked cruiser.

They switched to a dead baby in Queens. Someone had left the infant in a Dumpster, and they showed an EMS technician carrying the black body bag away with one hand, his face repressing anger at the camera crew. Who else was there to get angry at? Peggy thought. They would eventually bring in the suspects, the killers, the monsters, and, whoever they were, they would have a pathetic tale of woe; but in the end, who else was there to blame for this endless scroll of misery? Even the baby killers—the people who committed the worst crimes imaginable—would glare at the television camera, as if the crime itself, no matter how bad, did not measure up to the exposure. To the oppressive, demoralizing, and gloomy effect of the perpetual narrative of a malignant world peeled open and exposed.

Meanwhile, Mickey was rolling up his sleeve, still watching the screen.

"C'mon!" he grunted. "C'mon! C'mon!"

Peggy sighed and reached into the shopping bag and took out a glassine envelope.

"What is it?" he demanded.

"It's called King Kong," she said.

"Yeah, yeah! I heard about it. Very good. Very strong. C'mon, willya!"

"Turkish," she said.

She emptied the brown powder into a large soup spoon and diluted it with a few drops of water.

"Careful!" he yelled, seeing a few specks of the powder get loose. He was winding his belt around his arm. Peggy looked and saw the track marks. They were worse. He was dangerously far gone. She thought, This is going to be easy.

After heating the solution with four matches, Peggy loaded the heroin into the needle. The training at the pharmacy, along with some courses at the hospital where she studied to become a technician, made her competent with drugs and needles. Mickey's hand was trembling, and she had to be the one to insert the point of the needle into the vein. She drew back some blood, and Mickey started talking.

"You know, I quit the fucking job because of you."

His eyes were glued to the barrel of the hypodermic, watching the blood fill the tube, mix with the brown heroin, then plunge back into his arm.

"I couldn't handle that shit," he said, laughing and talking, talking and laughing. "The guys, they was always, you know, and I, well, you know the kind of guy I am . . ." He was sweating and crying and pumping his other hand, as if that would make the process go faster. His gibbering, she knew, was something to distract her from the ethical considerations. His and hers.

"This is all your fault, you know? You know that? I'm gonna hafta teach you a good lesson. First, I don't believe you about fuckin' around. Second, we gotta do something to those people."

He meant the TV people. She knew exactly what he meant.

"They said that I was useless! Useless!" He looked up, and in spite of the false laughter, his eyes were filled with tears and his face was twisted with anguish; if she hadn't made the decision that she made when she went up to the needle exchange and *copped* for him, Peggy would have felt some pity for Mickey. As it was, she was the one who felt the serene relief from the jolt of heroin that disappeared into her ex-husband's arm and soothed him.

"Oh!" he said, experiencing the first stage of the effects of the drug, when all feeling and all trouble were sucked out of his body.

She watched as he made one woozy try to loosen the belt. But he couldn't manage it. He swayed and was gone. The double dose of the drug had gone to work instantly. He fell back onto the pillows in a deep, narcotic sleep. Peggy waited a moment, listening to his heavy breathing. Gradually, it turned shallow. He made a few sounds—the deep protest of some primitive instinct. Out of his mouth a rope of drool began to unwind down the side of his face.

She reached over and took the remote control and changed the channel. Perhaps another news station would carry the story.

The tail end of the story was on Channel Seven. Somehow, it didn't come out right. They didn't tell the story. No one could. No one would. There was that policewoman again. She didn't care. No one cared. Peggy O'Neill put her own toxic spin on her ordeal:

Kevin Grant wouldn't listen. All he wanted to hear were the flashy, telegenic parts. No one wanted to hear the true, mud-ugly details of an abusive relationship. The truth was too pathetic, too gruelingly painful. They would listen if you were the brutal party. For that there was always an audience. Tell us how you beat and kicked and punched the woman you married.

If she cheated on her husband—if she *really* cheated, rather than the made-up cheating—then they would know and she would get an audience.

She realized with the slow-burning fuse of a deep rage that she was truly and completely alone. There was no one on her side.

And she was convinced that she had committed an overt act, possibly murder. She had bashed in that homeless woman's head with a rock. When the reckoning came there would be no pity for her. And she had tried to hide the act. She and Mickey had weighted down the black garbage bag with that rock and dumped it into the East River, but she knew well enough that bags broke and property would float to the surface and divers would go down sooner or later and retrieve the rock. Maybe her fingerprints would be on it. Maybe her DNA.

They would catch and handcuff her and she would be walked past the cameras and they would shout questions at her—and she would suffer a kind of media stoning.

Without any support. Mickey would turn against her if he could. He could cite the TV show on which she confessed her affair. He would point to her fingerprints on the rock. Mickey was her enemy.

Mel Carr would sell the book and movie rights to her story.

Peggy reached inside the shopping bag and pulled out the eight-inch-long, thick hatpin that she had bought at the antique hat shop on Third Avenue. She looked over and gazed at Mickey, curled in his fetal triumph on the bed, a hypodermic needle sticking out of his right arm, the tourniquet belt still tightened along the muscle.

Peaceful.

She walked closer and bent down and touched him. He did not budge. She could hear him breathing, she could see his stomach rise and fall, but he felt nothing. Of that she was certain. She took the hatpin and jabbed his finger. The reflexes were dull. Then she put her left hand behind his head and held it steady. He was lying on his right side, facing the window. His left eye was accessible.

"Mickey!" she cooed, and then, holding his head firm, she aimed the hatpin at the eye. First she touched the lid. Nothing happened. It was a stout weapon and she pushed against the handle of the pin with all her might. The hatpin bent, then rolled off the eyeball and followed a path along the occipital cavity, bouncing off the occipital bone, passing through the lobe, and penetrating the brain. She felt the squishy give of the brain as the hatpin passed through. It kept going until it struck the occiput. As it hit the back part of the skull, Mickey's eye suddenly opened, ripping through the lid. Mickey's arms and legs straightened for a second—a minor spasm—and he seemed to look at Peggy through his bleeding eye.

"I'm busy," she said to her now dead ex-husband.

She pulled the hatpin out of his eye. It took some effort. A small spill of blood followed.

EIGHT

Friday, January 13

Kevin Grant bolted off the set like a thief. His explanation was a breezy and painted lie. He said that it was something new to tickle the sense of excitement, to goose the sagging television talk-show format, to leave behind a whiff of high adventure.

As if they needed more excitement!

The truth was that he had been jolted by the phone call that came in during the first commercial break. When the stage manager yelled and held up the receiver, Kevin Grant was surprised. He shook his head angrily. Who calls in the middle of a taping? The stage manager was persistent, waving that receiver over his head like a dog shaking a bone, and mouthing that the call was *important*. Kevin Grant walked over, scowling, and snatched the phone from the stage manager's hand.

The woman on the other end of the phone introduced herself—Detective Lieutenant Maggie Van Zandt—and asked if she could interview him. She spoke in the flat, fortified voice of someone coming through the door. He had no real choice in the matter. He was going to talk to her.

"Will you be in your office in an hour, say, four?"

He started to make up an excuse. "I'm in the middle of taping a show!"

"I'll be there at four." She hung up before he could work out an extension.

The phone call was not entirely unexpected. Not after last night's alert from the mayor's wife, Ginny Shawn. The detective wanted to talk to him about that guest. That woman. The one who had trouble with her ex-husband and then was dragged out of her office. Abducted, the tabloid newspapers said. If you could believe them. Now the woman was missing. That word, *missing,* sent shivers down his back. It was his belief that very few people came back from that category.

Not that he felt any guilt. After all, it wasn't Kevin Grant who dragged her out of her little Queens office and made her missing. Still, why the hell didn't she just turn up? It was all that mystery that made it exhausting. He hated mystery. He wanted everything settled. That's why he went into television in the first place. Everything done at the end of the day. No homework.

He prayed—not that he believed in any version of God, unless it was some ultimate, all-powerful TV executive—that the poor woman would turn up safe. Even if she was hurt, even if she was black and blue, that would be all right, that could be fixed. They could get the show to put her up in a hotel. Putting someone up in a hotel always sounded generous. They could build up some audience sympathy, interest in a running story of the poor woman's plight. Abused women were hot. Have the husband on the show, too. Call it an intervention. Cure the son of a bitch on the air. Send them both for counseling. That would take the curse off the original sin, answer once and for all the exploitation complaint.

After that worrying phone call, Kevin Grant tried to remember Tuesday's show. Three days. God, he couldn't even remember the woman's face. If she was standing there on the set today, he wouldn't recognize her. The only thing that Kevin Grant remembered about her was that she was a complete dud on the air. A fizzle. She was supposed to toss a live grenade into the program about getting even with her abusive husband. But she turned out to be one of those prunes who dry up under the hot TV lights.

There are lots of them who see the camera and turn pale and go completely silent. Can't speak. Happens. And you can't always tell. Sometimes they look great on paper and they sound terrific in the preinterview. (He remembered that the assistant producer was all crazy and pacing after the preinterview, saying that she was gonna come out and denounce her old man, describe in detail the beatings and infidelities, and then the real eye-popping heart-stopping clincher, the payback—she would say that she got even with the bastard by cheating with a younger guy.)

Grant remembered a wild, wild look in the assistant producer's eyes. Get this, get this! She's gonna say all this for the first time on the air. The old man's gonna find out about it while watching the show! How's that for hot TV?

It should be a fuckin' rocket, said the snot-nosed, wild-eyed AP; get the beast out of their seats (that's what they called the audience: the beast) screaming, pumping those fists in the air in that Arsenio victory roll, making that savage, creepy audience animal hoot.

You had to trust the APs. Grant didn't like it, but, then, he didn't feel right about so much of this stuff. These kids who ran the show had that rock-and-roll cockiness. Live-wire confidence. They understood television. It was their thing. TV, on-line, virtual reality—same techno bullshit. He had to trust them. They were straight out of Harvard and Yale and Princeton—jacked up on Ivy League credentials and in-your-face conviction. They wore earrings and ponytails and talked about bitchin' after-hours clubs on the West Side of Manhattan where heroin was a kind of macho cocktail; they had waterfront lifestyles straight out of hell. They were in touch with the culture, and Kevin Grant was riding this talk-show tiger and took their word for it all.

Fact is, Grant was almost grateful when that woman sputtered out on the air. Poor woman—Peggy O'Neill. She was a mouse. She had that cringing smile, as if she were sorry all the time. When she folded, the AP just shook his hairy head and said, "Fuck it, fuck it, get past it, man." You can't come onto this stage cringing. You had to strut that Mick Jagger chicken strut and give the camera that fuck-you pucker and grab the microphone as if it were alive.

Just another washout and, in fact, Grant did forget about it. Still forgot about it. Could not remember shit. Now the phone call, and the cops wanted to talk to him, and he went through the rest of the day's taping in a blaze of stage fright. Felt flame in his ears.

Well, truth is, he always expected trouble. Not necessarily from this particular woman—he would have thought that the trouble, whatever form it came in, would come from one of those preteen, nasally sluts who didn't even know whose baby was inside their bellies. Trouble would come from some street psycho who would whip out a pistol on the air. He was braced for that.

They were playing with fire. There had to be a price to pay for all those messy, low-class triangles; for presenting all those sullen, street-corner outlaws; for searching out all those dumber-than-rock little girls hanging on to sullen adolescent gangsters; for showing sympathy to all those faded, jaded mothers sleeping with their daughters' pimply boyfriends—there would come an immense moral invoice for the biblical transgressions they pumped out into America.

This was, after all, the cost of success. Now, when it was too late, Kevin Grant suspected that he was much better off as a television ne'er-do-well, drifting from one small media market to the next until he could say—as he did with his signature joke—that he had gone national, one city at a time.

Well, it was hardly tragic. That's what you get when you have no talent beyond pale geniality: a safe, sunny vocation.

He had enough poise to sit in balmy, unwrinkled attendance on domesticated stage sets, filling up only space, during a range of dull daytime shows. It was a pleasant and dreamy life. No demands, no real strain. He lived in detached and lonely contentment. He married a few times (always to bleached, conspicuous beauties who were, without exception, approaching the far frontiers of their fleeting charms) but the unions were without real enthusiasm and inevitably ended in a fog of disappointment. Not rancor. Never hostility. Just a thicket of confusion.

Then, one day, he stood before the makeup mirror of his bleak and run-down dressing room in a third-rate Buffalo station and made the usual inventory of flesh, bone, hair, makeup, and wardrobe. He saw a clear picture of a man on the cusp of fifty, facing the end of the long, sweet glide of youth. Trembling in the mirror were the loose jowls and sagging eyelids of his own sealed fate. He beheld age.

And as he looked at the aging face in the dressing-room mirror, Kevin Grant knew that he had to make a move.

The timing was perfect. In the twilight of the twentieth century, America had become a culturally toxic wasteland. Every conventional mooring and authority had come unglued. Religion was discredited, politicians were one step ahead of the sheriff, entertainment heroes were either in rehab or denial, family elders were shut away in retirement homes. And so the unchecked voice of the television prophet stepped into the void with a strange new gizmo: psychobabble talk shows.

It was a high-tech miracle. Out of the pit of American misfits came unrepentent murderers, defrocked priests, anti-Semitic scholars, misunderstood Nazis. The bookers and audience coordinators ran amok, filling the seats with self-absorbed sex junkies, food junkies, enabler junkies, junk junkies, as well as the wide spectrum of abusers. In a pinch, they could always produce a recovering celebrity (from bulimia, alcohol, drugs, depression, career dips).

Nothing had to be borne stoically. And Kevin Grant was perfect for a host, with his ripe, long-suffering, pained presence.

At first, he asked himself why a reasonable person would expose the most intimate, ugly secrets to the world? In the end, he decided that it was to receive his (Kevin Grant's) blessing. It was his job to absorb every last vice and grievance, then finally, inevitably, issue the mild reproach of an arched eyebrow. He was to bestow TV amnesty: We hear your pain. We understand your weakness. We forgive your villainy. We loathe you—sympathetically.

It was said, in those private corporate meetings in which station managers assessed "talent," that Kevin Grant did his job, such as it was. He avoided large-scale scandal, he made certain that he did not offend the audience or disgrace the owners, he had no awkward personal habits or inhibiting scruples, and—this was the deciding factor—he had a deep respect for an open microphone.

Within six months of his debut, he was recognized as a safe and reliable pilot for the syndicator's show. The coarse performances raged all around him without disturbing his television poise. He ended the shows with a smile and an intake of air, suggesting sadness—and hope.

And he married again. Not just another ornament. This time he married a woman of some large media stature—someone to match, even enhance, his new standing. Judy Winner was the famous television psychologist Dr. Judy. She was, at the time of their union, a household name. They met when he was doing a show on incest and she was the guest expert. The subject of the show was unimportant. What mattered was something detected by the omniscient camera, seen before he knew it. It was a giddy flirtation in the midst of incest. Sparks flew, chemistry was beheld; Kevin and Judy became a dizzying and, in the words of *People* magazine, *happening* couple.

They were soon seen together at all the exclusive, tedious events—awards shows, openings, charity fashion galas. They were photographed holding hands before ducking into limousines and at first-night appearances. They got the best tables at the best restaurants. They flew first class.

But in spite of all this high privilege and splendor, there were nights when Kevin Grant awoke in a sweat. The show seemed to career beyond his comprehension. Don't push it, he told the assistant producers, as if their jobs didn't depend on pushing the envelope of sensation.

Gary Lock came out of the same middle-market abyss as Kevin Grant. Not quite thirty, Lock was the senior assistant producer of the talk show.

"Shouldn't we be more responsible?" Grant suggested to Lock from time to time.

"Hey, man, we are doing verbal gore," the senior assistant producer answered when Kevin Grant persisted. "You wanna go Oprah? You ain't Black enough or female enough. Take what you can get."

After eight months of big-time, syndicated testing, Gary Lock had other offers and could afford to mouth off.

During the last commercial break, after completing the show, Kevin Grant noticed the tabloid headline. He grabbed the newspaper out of the hands of a floor manager and read it on the run. The banner headline read, "Talked to Death." There was a picture of a woman—the caption said that she had been a guest on Tuesday's show. Peggy O'Neill. Tuesday's show? Christ! He stopped and read the text:

> A guest on Tuesday's The Kevin Grant Show *was apparently murdered after revealing on the air that she had had an extramarital affair. The sensational revelation apparently so unhinged her ex-husband that he dragged Peggy O'Neill out of the office in Queens where she worked as a paralegal, then cut her to pieces.*
>
> *The woman's body was found yesterday near the Great Lawn in Central Park. She was identified through a purse found in a garbage can just outside the Fifth Avenue entrance to the park. Police said that the dead woman had been too badly mutilated to identify by the usual means.*

The dead woman was a guest on the tabloid TV talk show
The Kevin Grant Show *on Tuesday, where she revealed that*
she had cheated during an abusive marriage. Police are now
searching for her ex-husband, Mickey O'Neill, 38, a limousine
driver.

He started to run for the shelter of the dressing room. "Great show," said Gary Lock, trailing closely as Kevin Grant fled. Lock ran to keep up. He had to be there to take the sweat-soaked towel that Kevin handed blindly over his shoulder.

Grant rushed ahead, avoiding the backstage crew, who watched with the critical malice of experts who knew how this particular trick worked. He ducked and danced between the coiled cables; he scrambled up the bare metal staircase, making his way to the star dressing room.

The air conditioner pumped and yet his face felt blistered. The makeup melted. He ripped off his shirt. He was too impatient to unbutton it and the destruction gave him a momentary lift. It was the exhilaration of battlefield waste.

"You want me to get you something to eat?" asked Gary Lock.

Kevin Grant shook his head. "The cops are coming," he said dramatically.

"So?"

He held out the newspaper.

Gary Lock had obviously seen it before. He looked at the newspaper, didn't bother to read it, then tossed it on the couch. "So?"

At that instant, Kevin Grant thought that getting lucky was the worst break he ever got.

NINE

It was never quiet at the Gotham. Peggy O'Neill sat up through the night trying to plot some kind of deliverance. But she could never fully concentrate. There were trucks grinding through the streets at off hours; there was music pounding from a dozen other rooms in a dozen different rhythms and styles; there were cries of pain and cries of ecstasy, sometimes attached to the same event. She could never quite gather her thoughts without that partial distraction.

She didn't even know what she was listening for. A sign. A clue. A trail. But all she heard was the fretful unrest of the city and the wind blowing through the crack in the window. At least the cold would keep the body on the bed from rotting.

As the sun came up, she felt the first tingle of alarm. She would have to do something soon. She would have to act. In the past, she could simply react to Mickey's demands. But now she was alone.

Then, with a heavy sigh, she spoke to the corpse: "You know, you were right." It was the first time she had ever addressed her ex-husband without worrying about provoking a blowback of dangerous anger. It was nice. She almost felt lightheaded. "There weren't many times in your life when you were ever right, Mick, but this time, you were dead right."

She was referring to his cry for vengeance. Getting even with the television people for leading her on. It was, she thought, the right thing to do. And yet, she had no tactical plan. All she had was an emotion, an idea, without form or aim. But in that cold hotel room with the dead body of her ex-husband lying on the bed, she began to think of a way to carry out one more righteous murder.

Peggy O'Neill phoned Dr. Judy Winner's office from an open booth on Fifth Avenue. The receptionist on the other end of the line was frazzled.

"She cannot come to the phone," said the receptionist sharply.

"I'm with *Modern Women* magazine," said Peggy O'Neill, who plucked the name off a newsstand. "Could I just speak to Dr. Winner for one moment?"

The receptionist, who was at the end of her endurance, closed her eyes. "You will have to go through the public-relations firm that handles Dr. Judy's publicity, madam."

There were photographers and makeup artists and lighting specialists running back and forth at the Seventy-eighth Street office. The receptionist's chair was in the way, and so they simply moved it. The receptionist stood with the phone in her hand and her temper at a volatile pitch. Someone in the crew had just taken away her coffee.

"And who handles her publicity?" asked Peggy O'Neill.

"Pine and Cohen." The receptionist spoke through clenched teeth.

"You don't happen to have their phone number handy?"

"Look it up," said the receptionist, laying the receiver in the cradle, resisting the urge to smash it down and break it, then run screaming out onto Second Avenue.

An hour later, Peggy O'Neill walked into the offices of Pine & Cohen, Ltd., on West Forty-fourth Street in Midtown. She was met by a smartly dressed blonde young woman, Janet Myers, who seemed a little disappointed.

"You're the lady from *Modern Women?*" asked the young woman.

Peggy nodded.

Janet Myers was dangerously excited. In spite of the fact that she had only been on the job for six weeks, the twenty-six-year-old assistant account executive at the public-relations firm of Pine & Cohen, Ltd., decided that she could handle this media pitch on her own. After all, it was only the simple vending of a client to a magazine. All she had to do was hand over a packet of Dr. Judy Winner's bio material and clips to the researcher from *Modern Women* magazine and act reasonably civil. No hard sell required. No big deal. The piece was presold. At least that was the impression she was given by the woman, who identified herself as a researcher over the phone.

Ordinarily, it would have been her boss, Mary Lester, the senior account executive, who would deal directly with the press— offering a refreshment, presenting the glad-handing resources of her trade with smiles and gestures in order to leave behind the slight but certain tracks of goodwill and professional obligations. That's what they did in the PR game—they laid down liabilities with every service.

In the short span of time that she had been in the PR game, the ambitious and alert Janet Myers had watched carefully how her boss operated. She saw the clever way that the senior account executive controlled the spin of a story by employing the whole range of enabling skills—arranging an interview, suggesting a tack, cautioning against forbidden topics, faking enthusiasm, providing angles, spare change for the telephone. Mary Lester would even equip a lazy journalist with a pad and pen.

However, at the moment, Mary Lester was out of the office. She was babysitting the client, Dr. Judy Winner, who was posing for an important color publicity shoot for *TV Guide*. They were staging the shoot in Dr. Judy's own dramatically earth-toned clinical office in order to achieve what everyone called a closer touch of reality. Good thing that Mary Lester was on the scene, too. The delicate temperament of the famous psychologist was wound unusually tight by her husband's sudden tabloid connection to a missing TV guest.

The senior publicist correctly anticipated that her soothing presence was required during the photo shoot, for she knew that the tightly wound psychologist was always one crisis away from her own mental breakdown.

Thus Janet Myers was left behind holding the fort. Smiling, she ushered Peggy O'Neill, posing as a magazine researcher, into the twelfth-floor conference room of Pine & Cohen, Ltd. For reasons of antique sentiment, the offices of the firm were located in the original home of the *New Yorker* magazine on West Forty-fourth Street. Literary ghosts were said to bolster the firm's credibility.

In spite of the fact that she had been left in charge of the office, Janet nevertheless had a moment of doubt about her license to act. She excused herself from the waiting researcher and, from another remote office, phoned her boss.

Thirty-four blocks north and a few city avenues to the east of the public-relations office, Mary Lester was trying to cope with the colliding egos and impossible demands of a tribe of temperamental aesthetes. Dr. Judy's office had been transformed, draped in white sheets to enhance the light. The high-intensity strobes were straining the electrical circuits. The makeup artists were ready; the photographer wasn't. The costume designers complained of wilted fabric. The photographer wanted a more vivid image, while Dr. Judy preferred a muted picture. No one was happy.

Standing off in a corner, Mary Lester listened with seething impatience to her assistant explain the small emergency caused by the sudden interest of a magazine. Then, quietly, in a voice hissing with suppressed emotion, Mary Lester explained to her assistant that she was juggling a moody photographer, a hypersensitive stylist, a waspish makeup artist, and a pair of thin-skinned clothing designers. In an even softer, more menacing tone, she reported that the list of critical-care patients included a paranoid client. Over the crackling, unsteady cellular connection, she directed her assistant to deal with whatever it was that had come up—hand over material, assemble a press kit, promise an interview—she had a real crisis on her hands.

Janet Myers was delighted. Buoyed by this jolt of confidence, she walked back to the conference room, which was when she made her first big mistake: She didn't ask the dull, dusty woman who came to pick up the bio material for her press credentials. It was a matter of squeamishness. She didn't want to insult the poor thing. Peggy O'Neill looked nothing like the usual glamorous literary and electronic news media acolytes who came sniffing after a story. This one was a heavy, wet presence. She had a flat unlovely face and wore an inelegant hat that looked like a lump of unformed clay.

"Some tea?" suggested Janet Myers.

Not hearing an outright refusal, the aspiring publicist turned to the high counter, where she fussed with the pot of hot water and some cups and the tea bags, puzzled by the plainness of the researcher. "Hope you don't mind Earl Grey."

From the corner of her eye she watched the researcher staring down at her lap, not even bothering to absorb the intentionally tacky decor of the office. The walls of the conference room were willfully disfigured by signed pictures of second- and third-level celebrity clients—third-string local politicians, unsuccessful authors, fading singers, climbing socialites, down-at-the-heels character actors. Mary Lester called it "a hoot."

Janet Myers took a seat across the large oak table. She handed a spoon to the guest, poured an artificial sweetener into her own tea, and felt a blush of satisfaction: She had the upper hand. That was the key, according to Mary Lester—always get the upper hand.

"So, what do you think you're going to do?" she asked brightly, tossing a flourescent smile across the table.

"I, uh . . .," began the researcher.

The woman was bewildered. The researcher was new to this

end of the business, Janet Myers told herself. She had probably spent a lifetime working the phones, delving into files, fact-checking tiny, unimportant details. She took a closer look, and it surprised her that the researcher was not so very old. Then Janet Myers made her second mistake. Instead of challenging the competence of the researcher, instead of seeing the inappropriate and odd demeanor for what it was—a determined act of deceit—she saw it as an opportunity, a chance to influence an approach from an important magazine.

"I'm sure you want to do some sort of profile," she said brightly, helpfully. "It certainly is a ripe time for a profile on Dr. Judy. She's such a rich subject."

"Yes. Yes. Of course," said the woman in the shapeless hat and thick winter coat.

"Probably the 'Woman of the Month' feature," offered Janet Myers. "Balancing family and career. Trying to have a baby. Her famous husband and her own blossoming reputation; these are very hard things to handle, as you and I know. . . ."

Janet Myers went on with her promotional soliloquy, not noticing that the face of the researcher was clouded with disinterest and confusion.

". . . But Dr. Judy's a very spunky lady. Great material for an in-depth feature. You know, I don't think that anyone's ever done a real in-depth piece about her before. Just superficial, admiring stuff. You know, fluff."

She laughed, suggesting that fluff was beneath the standards of the researcher's magazine.

"Yes," agreed the researcher haltingly, leafing through the prepared handouts and files of clippings. "Of course . . . I think it might help . . . to focus things . . . if I could meet Dr. Winner."

"Dr. Judy," corrected Janet Myers in a honeyed voice. "Please call her Dr. Judy. She doesn't even like using the title of doctor." She laughed. "Sounds too pretentious." She waved her hand in the air. "Not that she isn't entitled to it. Many honors. Many degrees. As you can see . . ." She pointed to the academically bulked-up CV, the publicist's steroid package of material.

Peggy O'Neill nodded in agreement. She turned to Janet Myers with a little more force. "I need to speak to her—get, you know, a line on something and then we could . . . you know . . ."

"Set something up?"

Peggy nodded emphatically. "That would be perfect. I have some time tomorrow."

Janet Myers frowned. It was an unusual facial expression in the offices of Pine & Cohen. "Weekends are sacred," she said in what she hoped was a sorrowful voice. "It's the only time she can spend with her family."

"There is a Monday story conference. . . . I wanted to be able to . . ." She paused.

"Yes." Janet Myers shook her head. She had been drilled in the iron rule: no weekend appointments. "But almost any other time. You see, tomorrow she's got an appointment for some fittings at Saks. It's the only time she has, really."

"Well, that's that," said the drab woman in the ugly hat, who started to gather up her material. Suddenly, she seemed clear and filled with purpose.

"Well, could we arrange something for . . . maybe some time next week?" suggested Janet Myers.

"I'll call you," said the researcher.

It was abrupt. Janet Myers thought she had said or done something to insult the researcher. The junior publicist felt the story—her first true assignment—slipping away.

"You know," she said airily, "she's such an interesting person. I could tell you stories all day. She volunteers in a food kitchen. Of course that's off-the-record. She doesn't like to parade her charities. And she's always bringing in boxes of chocolates." She leaned closer. "She has a weakness for chocolate."

"Really?" said the researcher.

"Dark chocolate." Janet Myers nodded. "Can't resist. Even when she brings in a box for us, she steals one."

They both laughed. "I like chocolate," said the researcher.

Janet Myers felt the solid common ground return beneath her feet. "Me, too; but if I don't watch myself I'd have to be in the gym all day."

Finally, she asked if she could expect a call early in the week from the researcher. The researcher nodded.

They parted outside, in the hall, in front of the elevator. Janet Myers thought that she had done well. Slipped a bit, but saved the day. The researcher smiled, but kept her face averted, and agreed with the chirping publicist about almost everything.

Her thoughts were not on the possibility of doing a flattering story about Dr. Judy Winner. She had heard enough. She now had a precise plan to kill the good Dr. Judy.

TEN

The stocky young man waiting at the reception desk of the Global Television Network on West Sixty-seventh Street slouched insolently against the counter. He had a disagreeable frown on his face as he looked Maggie and Sam up and down. "I guess you're the cops," he said unpleasantly.

Maggie turned to Sam, who shrugged, then turned back to the stubby young man. The show of such quick malice was unusual. She was accustomed to deference. She fished her gold detective's shield out of her purse. "We are the cops," she admitted gently. "I take it that you are from *The Kevin Grant Show*?"

He didn't respond, just turned, and said in that same flat voice, "Follow me."

"Hold it," she said, moving quickly in front of his path, blocking the way. "I know who we are. Who are you?"

He smiled; it was not a friendly smile. "I'm Gary Lock," he said, "the senior production assistant. It's a title that doesn't begin to convey my real power."

Maggie laughed. Maybe he was just trying to be funny. "I have the same problem with the shield," she replied good-naturedly. "However, I do have the handcuffs and the gun as a backup."

"I'm really impressed."

Now there was no mistaking the whiff of gunpowder in the air. Maggie shook her head. Sam shrugged again. "He could be working for the chief," whispered Sam. "You know, trying to thwart an interview with Kevin Grant by being very obnoxious."

"Nah," said Maggie, indicating the assistant. "He's too short to be on the job. Still, you never know how far the boss'll go to impress a celebrity friend of the mayor's wife."

She did have to consider the other possibility—that this was New York City, the global headquarters of rude behavior, and naked animosity was simply Gary Lock's typical style. Then Maggie had another thought. The senior production assistant could be deflecting the prospective heat away from his star, Kevin Grant. He was acting as a lightning rod. If true, it was a truly noble gesture, thought Maggie generously.

The youth led them into a coffin-sized elevator. "Private," he said. That meant it was close and sluggish and airless. They rode up without breathing. On the fourth floor, they discharged like an exhaled breath into a great empty bay. As they advanced into the hangerlike space of the studio, Maggie saw that in spite of the sense of vacant size, the bay was quite busy. There was a portion sectioned off for a news set, another for a situation comedy, a chunk put aside for a weather map. And dappled among the sets were lights and cables and microphone booms.

The sets were bracketed by portable bleachers for the audience. And all of it, every set and stick, was absorbed by the immense size of the studio. Very useful space, Maggie thought. It could be opened or shrunk to suit the need. Like putting partitions in an office. Then, out of the shadows, she heard the swish and murmur of people stirring, moving scenery, shifting cameras, resetting lights.

"Boy!" said Sam.

Maggie was impressed. All those television men wheeling around big cameras and thick cables and heavy lights—like cowboys twirling trick lariats. Showing off. She'd seen cops use the same gimmick with their guns—letting lethal weapons slap up against their hips, as if deadly power were an ordinary, everyday thing. She had, herself, made use of offhand, insinuated power, letting the thick walls of the station house and the windowless interrogation rooms and the steel bars of the holding pens do the heavy lifting of breaking down a witness.

She turned and whispered to Sam, "Don't lose your head."

Sad Sam nodded. "Right," he said.

She knew that it was very glamorous, very tingly and exciting to be at the very core of a great media empire where they could run into all sorts of talented and important people. It had an intoxicating impact. "Remember," she said to Sam, "we're the cops."

"That's who we are, okay. We are the official cops," he repeated softly. "So how come we're following that nasty little troll?"

He nodded off at the bumpy little assistant, who seemed to be rushing ahead, almost power-walking. "Because he is taking us to his leader."

Gary Lock, Maggie suspected, could probably grant or deny television life. That kind of authority could turn someone into a mean little kid, she believed.

Picking up the pace, Gary Lock forced them to speed up.

Maggie had her own tactical gifts. She stopped cold and looked around at the inside of the studio, as if she were studying the terrain. The assistant acted as if he had the leash and Maggie had to follow, and he kept walking at his pace. Sam paused at a mediating halfway point. He could see the thunderhead of trouble brewing. Finally, the assistant stopped, turned, and put his hands on his hips, waiting.

Maggie stood in front of an empty row of bleachers.

"So this is where they shoot the show?" she asked.

"Yes, this is where they shoot the show," Gary Lock replied. He used a mild singsong, as if to suggest that it was an idiotic question.

"The set looks different in person," she said, smiling. "Well, you know what they say: Television adds ten pounds."

"It looks different because there's no set." His voice bounced off the high ceilings. "They pull it down after the show and tape a game show. Then they put it back together in the morning."

"I knew it looked a little thin," said Maggie.

"Can't fool you."

Uh-oh, Sad Sam said to himself.

Maggie nodded, walking up to the youth. She shut down the charm and went into her all-business mode. "You've worked for him how long?"

"Eight months here. Couple of years before that in the hinterland. You wanna question me, too? 'Cause if you do, I wanna have a lawyer. And I want my Miranda warning."

She thought about that. Then she turned on her heel, grabbed Gary Lock under the right elbow, and yanked his elbow up quickly, shifting his weight, throwing him off balance, making him stumble. She kept moving against his center of gravity, so that he couldn't regain his balance; she took him out of the range of Sad Sam's hearing. Her hold was surprisingly powerful—a cop's iron grip—and the youth found himself helpless.

When she spoke, her voice carried a soft menace. "Listen, you have a perfect right to counsel and I am going to give you a little counseling. I have no idea what wild hair you have up your stumpy little ass, but ease up, pal. Don't push me, don't dis me, don't get in my way." She leaned even closer, pushing him, making his feet scramble to keep up with his falling body mass. " 'Cause if you fuck with me, junior, the only thing you will assistant-executive produce is a plea bargain." Then she released him and walked away. He staggered a bit, then stood straight, embarrassed, frightened.

Sad Sam walked over, leaned close, and whispered, "You've just had an official Maggie warning."

Gary Lock was confused.

"Mr. Grant must be getting a little impatient," she said, as if nothing had happened. "I'm sure he's a busy man and I don't want to keep him waiting."

Gary Lock paled, nodded, and brought Sam and Maggie to Kevin's office without another word.

Kevin Grant was tall and had a little more wear and tear than Maggie expected, but there was the unmistakable star presence. He was well-groomed and pampered and sleek. He wore expensive clothes and had a professional greeting. He was also nervous. "Please, please," he said, offering Maggie a soft chair. He was using the larger office of the station manager for the interview.

"One second," said Maggie; then she turned and issued discreet instructions to Sam.

"Take the kid around the block."

"Should I try to question him?"

"No. If he wants to talk, let him. But don't let him split. I wanna talk to him after I get through here. Give me half an hour."

Sam nodded and efficiently took charge of Gary Lock.

Kevin Grant recognized the command and authority of the woman in the soft leather chair. He didn't know how, but she had shaken Gary Lock—something he had never been able to do. The talk-show host, who was standing behind the desk, came around and sat across from Maggie on the sofa.

"This thing . . ." He was holding out the afternoon newspaper. "Is it really her?"

Maggie shook her head ambiguously. "Newspapers," she said dismissively. "They seldom get it right."

The story had shaken him. To Maggie, it was a good sign. He had a nice innocent quality. And he was ignorant about the media. Maggie saw that Kevin Grant had no idea about the whipsaw nature of the press. He thought that being a member of the fraternity—albeit the high-profile, high-paid show-business end—gave him some special status, a privileged rank, earned him some extra mileage when it came to the courtesies. She knew better. She understood that they would turn on him quicker, just to prove that they were impartial.

"Tell me about Peggy O'Neill," she said.

It was only a name. His memory was slippery, she saw. And he had a frightened look. She felt a momentary touch of pity.

"You know, it was odd," said Kevin Grant; his head was bent and he shook it back and forth.

"What was odd?"

"Her story. They told me about it. They always brief me about the guests." She nodded. "Can't let me go out there cold." He smiled, as if revealing a trade secret of the talk show gave them intimate common ground.

She was patient. Give them time. You got more information when the story emerged.

He ran his hand through his hair. "Well, they said that she had a rough marriage, which was the theme of the show. Brutal husbands. You know, we were going to try to stage some kind of intervention. Get them into therapy. We try not to be exploitive or use stories for the sake of shock value. There's social value in our show."

Maggie nodded. Not that she believed it, but she knew that you had to allow for the pride of people in a tight spot.

"But . . ." He shook his head.

"I saw the tape," she said. "You know what I found curious? You seemed to cut her short."

He nodded and smiled ruefully. "That's true. In fact, I really didn't want her to tell her story." His head was bent.

"Why not?"

He took his time answering. Looked around. "I just didn't believe her," he said finally.

This took Maggie by surprise. "Pardon me?"

"I just didn't think that she was the type. Not the beating part. I believed that. The other part. About cheating on her ex-husband. I didn't believe her when she said that she had an affair."

"You think she made it up?"

He leaned even closer; she could smell the expensive cologne, along with the sweat. "People do it all the time. To get on television. Sometimes you have to protect them from their own exaggerations." He smiled again sadly. "They want to be on television." He shrugged and coughed out a laugh.

ELEVEN

So quickly, she thought. It wasn't even five-thirty yet and already darkness was falling. Peggy O'Neill was not yet prepared for night. She still had important errands to run.

The streets were quick with icy pedestrians rushing in their huddled winter fashion to get out of the cold weather. She, herself, did not feel the weather. She felt only the warm urgency of her mission.

At Eighty-fifth Street, she stopped at a chain pharmacy and handed the clerk behind the counter a prescription. She had a bagful of prescription blanks, taken when she left the job at the pharmacy in Queens. She had filled one in while having an early dinner at one of the German restaurants on Eighty-sixth Street in Yorkville. Between the schnitzel and the spaetzle, she wrote down on the scrip a prescription for one hundred tablets of digoxin.

"We only have seventy-five tablets," said the clerk, an efficient young man who did not look up from the desk behind the counter. "I'll have to owe you twenty-five."

"That's fine," said Peggy. She wouldn't need more than a handful of the tablets anyway. She paid in cash, noting that she had $287 left from the money she had withdrawn from the bank.

"What's the name on this?" asked the clerk.

He held the prescription blank down from the high counter. "Ryan," said Peggy O'Neill. "Mrs. Mary Ryan."

"And the address?"

"That's twenty-five East Eighty-ninth Street," she said, making it up.

He wrote it down on the blank.

"And your age, Mrs. Ryan?"

"Sixty-two," she replied.

He wrote that down in the appropriate spot and handed her the plastic childproof tube. He didn't bother to glance over to see if the woman under his counter fit the age. She knew that he wouldn't examine her. She was protected by a shield of epidemic impersonality. Urbanites did not tread on anyone else's space. It was a tacit and essential agreement to keep the everyday encounters remote and safe. No one looked at anyone else on the subway. There were consequences to bumping a stranger on the street. Clerks made change without ever looking up from the cash register. Machines made bank transactions and answered phone questions without live interaction. It was an outgrowth of cyberspace and a great unspoken convenience to avoid bruising or lethal confrontations between unpredictable and explosive humans.

Suddenly, Peggy felt at one with the modern ethos. She, too, lived in the shadows of solitary and detached evasion. She, too, harbored wild secrets behind the mask of indifference.

She headed back downtown, the tablets and the other materials in her bag. There was a cold, wet snow falling. It melted as soon as it hit the Manhattan sidewalk. Peggy felt her hat grow soggy as she walked. She didn't mind. She didn't mind the water seeping into her boots and soaking her feet. What did it matter? She would do what she had to do in a matter of days. All time and all arrangements were now compressed into hours. If she caught a cold, it didn't affect the simple plan. If she had blisters or moments of distress, it was not worth bothering about. Nothing had any long-range implications.

Sad Sam was back from his walkabout with Gary Lock, waiting outside of the station manager's office. He had an odd, worried expression on his face when Maggie poked her head out of the door. The sullen kid producer stood behind him, arms folded across his chest, sending out sparks instead of flames.

"What's the weather like?" she asked.

"Rain," said Sam, turning his head, indicating something over his shoulder. "House full of trenchcoats."

She nodded. The press. She guessed that they would be downstairs in the lobby. They were there for Kevin Grant, not for her. She decided to leave, get back to the cop house. An open, undefended TV studio was too exposed. "I'm gonna take the kid. And Grant. I'll be at the Nineteenth."

The Nineteenth Precinct station house was located on Sixty-seventh Street; close enough to Midtown to stay in touch with the task force and higher command, yet away from the media squall.

"Meet me there," she added. "Send someone out to Queens. I wanna talk to that lawyer again. . . ."

"Carr?"

"Carr." She nodded.

"Meet me at the One Nine."

Maggie wanted to get Gary Lock back into her own environment. Getting Kevin Grant away from the studio was a favor. She felt some sympathy for the man. It was always that way in an investigation. She formed opinions, attachments, developed a rooting interest, felt the bloom of unexpected affection. Or else a quick repugnance. She called it the aesthetic of the case. It couldn't be helped. Not that it would stop her from doing her job. She had lost count of the number of times when she had had to clap handcuffs on someone she had prematurely declared her protagonist, or had set free her instant villain.

As she led Kevin Grant—hidden under a slouch hat and dark glasses—and Gary Lock out of the building, she could hear the urgent clamor of the reporters. She didn't want to attract attention, so they walked at a normal pace. Out of the corner of her eye she saw Sad Sam hold up his arm and cry out for silence.

"Just hold it! Hold it down!"

The Nineteenth Precinct on East Sixty-seventh Street was an old station house, sitting next to an Orthodox Jewish synagogue. It was a block away from Hunter College. On the walls and steps of the college sat a bewildering variety of students in a rainbow of tribal colors—foreign robes and peculiar headgear and outspoken buttons—like academic gang members declaring their multicultural affinity. The area was sprinkled with romantic foreign embassies and overpriced restaurants, so that, together with the college and the synagogue and unique shopping arcades, the street traffic had an exotic and wildly openhearted charm. Palestinian exchange students shared English-lit class notes with kids wearing yarmulkes; undercover cops flirted with social scholars. It was a perfect setting for a station house rendezvous. No one seemed out of place.

Maggie settled into an empty detective commander's office on the second floor of the precinct. She put Gary Lock in an empty interrogation room. After reassuring and settling Kevin Grant into a more comfortable office, she made a call to the coroner. It took him ten minutes to get back to her—he was busy with another postmortem—and he sounded rushed when he got on the line.

"The lady in the park," she said.

"What about her?"

"Do we have any kind of ID?"

"We have a very vague kind of ID. Female. Unknown. Somewhere between thirty-five and forty-five years old. Five feet two. About one hundred ten pounds. Poorly nourished."

"You can't tell what she had, say, for a last meal?"

He exhaled impatiently. "Very little. There was no food in her stomach, but, of course, she could have already digested her last meal. Oh, there was one thing: I can tell you that she was an alcoholic. There were a lot of secondary characteristics—malnourished, extensive liver damage. The blood alcohol level was high, 1.9. Certain muscle atrophy associated with chronic alcoholism. Lots of scrapes and cuts—not from the lethal attack, but the kind that comes from motor disfunction. Classic signs."

"You think she was younger than thirty-five?"

He thought about that. "I doubt it. In fact, no. Thirty-five is the cellar. She was probably a lot closer to forty-five. But, as I say, without some clinical history and with the body in such a bad way, I'll need more time. Toxicology, DNA. That takes time."

The lawyer, Mel Carr, was pacing in the bay of the detective command. He took Maggie aside. "I didn't know if I should tell you this because, well, it might fall under the umbrella of privileged communication."

"Really?"

"There are ethical considerations. But having thought about it, I decided to tell you. Miss O'Neill did not have an affair to get even with her husband."

Maggie did not react. She took the lawyer to her office, sat him down, had Sad Sam stand there as a witness, and made him repeat the story. "She said that someone on the show made her do it. It would make for a better TV show."

He looked around, seeking support. No one blinked.

Then Maggie asked him, "How much did she drink?"

"Who?"

"Peggy."

"You mean as a rule? As a rule, she drank exactly nothing." He looked around, as if he were faced with a trick question. "She hated liquor."

"Not even on the sneak."

He shook his head.

Gary Lock looked worried. Maggie read through a few reports, ignoring him. She was establishing her territorial supremacy.

The young senior production assistant was sensitive to the game and remained quiet. Without looking up, she spoke:

"What do you think? You think that Peggy O'Neill had an affair to get even with her husband?"

"I dunno? I guess so? That's what she said."

Maggie lifted a few papers, pretended to read. Then: "I don't think so. She wasn't the type."

"I, uh, can't believe that," he said.

She knew what she wanted to know.

With a sigh of resignation, she called Chief Scott, who was at Manhattan North Detective Command on Fifty-first Street.

"Where the hell are you?" he yelled.

"I'm working the talk-show case," she said. "I got a couple of things that need checking. Let me poke around for a while. I'll tell you why, boss. You know the lady in the park? It ain't that talk-show lady. The ME is very shaky about the ID. Couple of details sound a little wrong."

She hung up before she could hear him cry, "What the fuck am I going to tell the reporters?"

TWELVE

It was a shock. The woman waiting for the southbound bus on Lexington Avenue at Sixty-second Street turned and noticed her own reflection in the window of a gourmet food shop. Peggy O'Neill stood taller than she remembered, her head was held straighter, she looked years younger—her very presence radiated a kind of exotic confidence, even in the store window.

She laughed. The others waiting under the bus shelter took pains not to notice. People who spoke to themselves and laughed out loud in Manhattan were granted conditional immunity from strict social codes. No one wanted to provoke a street psycho. They just wanted psychos to hold out until a new jolt of medication kicked in or until they were personally out of range.

In her new undercover state of heightened awareness, Peggy recognized this odd phenomenon, depended on it. There was safety in a certain amount of reckless behavior.

It was crowded on the bus and she forced her way deep into the interior, pushing against the resolute passengers blocking the aisles. They might not goad a madwoman, but New York commuters on a southbound bus were not about to surrender a picked spot without a fight.

Peggy O'Neill battled past the people lost in the tabloid story of her vicious murder, through the cold, indifferent mass of the populace, most of whom went through the miserable voyage home half-lidded and riddled with dull office grief. They did not bother to look up or even notice Peggy O'Neill, who was beginning to glow in the aftermath of her tragic disappearance. After all, she had rematerialized in a gourmet food shop window as a completely different person.

The bus shivered and swerved to avoid a cab cutting across its bow to pick up a fare. Peggy had a momentary fear that she might spill the contents of her brown Bloomingdale's shopping bag. It would not be good if everyone on the bus saw the fresh hypodermic needle. Of course, she thought, in the style of her inventive new personality, it wouldn't really matter; they would all look away, embarrassed for having noticed.

She began to hum something tuneless, and the other passengers delicately created a space. Peggy felt safe in her new layer of wacky armor. She was capable of almost anything now, especially her great new plan.

Pudge Keene was running up the metal stairs to the anticrime unit in the Nineteenth Precinct station house when he almost collided with Lieutenant Maggie Van Zandt, who was heading the other way. The Man Murph was right behind Pudge and got caught in the pileup.

"Wanted to see you gentlemen," said Maggie, wagging a finger for them to follow.

Pudge looked confused. Murph took it in. "Wha's up, Lieutenant?"

She waited until Sad Sam was included in the group, then led them to the squad commander's office and closed the door. They were all standing, a signal that this was not a long, drawn-out thing. Maggie had something very specific and quick in mind. "The guy, what's his name?"

The two undercover cops looked confused. Maggie pressed: "The man with the purse."

"Oh, Nafume Benjamin," said Murph.

"Benjamin. Right. I wanna talk to him."

Pudge wrinkled his brow in thought. Murph smiled. "That's not easy, Lieutenant," said the Man.

"Why is that?" she asked crisply.

"Well, couple of things, Lieutenant; one, the guy's homeless," he pointed out. "You know what I'm sayin'? That means he ain't exactly got a doorbell."

"What's the other thing?"

"No other thing. That about covers the whole thing."

She ticked off points on her fingers. "Homeless guys have turf. They follow patterns. They dine at preferred soup kitchens. They bathe in friendly shelters. They sleep in congenial doorways. We know that this particular homeless gentleman has a territorial range that includes the south end of Central Park. We can speak to shopkeepers, hotel and apartment-house doormen, mail deliverers, cops. This is a security-sensitive area. Lots of rich people. Lots of eyes on the street. Someone will have noticed him. He is distinctive when it comes to haberdashery. A tall, moving mountain of rags, even in *laissez-aller* Midtown Manhattan, is bound to attract some attention."

"You want us to arrest him?" asked Pudge.

"No, of course not," said Maggie. "He's our favorite witness. I just wanna talk to him. He's a very bright man and he'll know the difference between a bust and a conversation. You may point out that there are certain advantages for his cooperation. Per diem, for example. And buy him a meal. Homeless guys like it when you show them a good time."

"Where?" asked Pudge, the dense, practical one.

"Where what?"

"Where should we buy him a meal?"

"Not Lutèce. Just a decent sandwich and a bowl of soup and then coax him in."

"Right," said Murph sheepishly. "What about our sergeant? We're supposed to be out nailing picks."

"What's your sergeant's name?"

"Sanders."

Maggie nodded at Sad Sam, who was writing the name of Sergeant Sanders, anticrime squad, on his pad.

"No sweat," she said. "You work for me until further notice. I'll talk to him."

"Her," said Murphy, with an immense smile. "Janet Sanders. And she be Black, too!"

"Get the fuck out of here and call in every hour," said Maggie, laughing along with Murph.

The neon lights had long since stopped working and a layer of soot almost obliterated the sign that proclaimed the Gotham Hotel. After leaving the bus on Park Avenue South, Peggy walked west to the hotel, checking to see that she wasn't followed. She had developed cunning habits, a detail which amused more than frightened her.

She nodded to the vaguely unfriendly clerk on the desk and climbed the two flights of stairs rather than risk the unreliable elevator. It was not a great effort. In her new persona, she had nothing but energy. All those years of weary and timid struggle were wiped away by this dying burst of strength and stamina.

The lock on 315 had been broken, and so it was hard to engage the bolt. Peggy jiggled the key until she got it to turn. The room was cold. The lights and television were on, as they had been when she left. Mickey was still in bed, his back turned to her, as if he were asleep. She placed the shopping bag on the table and sat down in the drooping stuffed chair with broken springs.

"It went fine," she announced proudly.

She looked over at the back of his body. She almost expected him to lumber back to life. Maybe even come at her. Hard to break that bad memory.

"I have plotted our revenge," she said brightly. "I spoke to the woman at the public-relations agency and she gave me an idea.

I won't tell you about it now. I'll make it a surprise. Just say that in order to carry out the idea I needed a few things. I was very imaginative. I went up to Yorkville, then Spanish Harlem and the place you sent me."

She spoke as if there were someone there to listen. It was not quite madness, she thought. She knew that Mickey O'Neill was dead. And she knew what she was doing. This was an exercise in religious expiation. An act of penance. She was evoking ancient rituals and memories of communion and recognition of church authority; she did not have to bear all the sins and sorrows alone. True, there was no priest to offer absolution, or to instruct her in the renunciation of Satan and his works. But there were amnesties and remissions of sins that were accepted in the absence of a priest.

The thought made her happy.

"I found the needle-exchange clinic. On Ninety-sixth Street. I waited outside until a woman came by and she looked very sick. I told her that I needed some help. She thought I was a policewoman."

Peggy laughed. "Well, I paid her for her dirty needles. I was afraid to go inside the clinic. I thought someone might recognize me. My picture has been in the newspapers. I gave her forty dollars. She was very grateful. Of course, she took my money and disappeared. She gave me the needles, though. You know, addicts are very paranoid."

Peggy laughed again. "Imagine! Of course you know."

She stared at the back of the man in the bed. He did not move. The room was badly lit. The only light came from a sixty-watt bulb. Better that way, she thought. Couldn't see all the vermin. That was the one thing she didn't like about the new life. The filth and the vermin.

"So, I went inside the clinic and got fresh needles. I was worried. You know, that they would question me. Ask for identification. Some proof that I was an addict. But they don't even ask. Not my name. Not anything. It's very easy to be an addict. I didn't know. After I got the needles I got some lunch. It was a German place. You'd have hated it. I really enjoyed the fact that you would have disliked it so much. There are so many things I enjoy now just because you hated them so much. Very wicked! Then I did a little shopping. I got the medication—shocking what you have to pay for drugs these days—then I bought some clothing and a box of chocolates."

She got up and removed her coat and walked over to the standing closet to put the coat away. She passed the bed and when she turned around, she smiled down at her ex-husband. There was a small trickle of blood coming out of his left eye, just as there had been when she left. And in the middle of the eye she could see the hole the long hatpin had made when she had plunged it into Mickey's brain.

He was beginning to smell, but Peggy poured alcohol and perfume over the corpse to lessen the odor.

"Not much longer; I have everything I need now," she said to the rotting remains of her ex-husband.

THIRTEEN

Maggie was exhausted. It was, of course, the ache in her jaw. It had turned ugly and kept her up at night. The pain was bearable—she could always take a high degree of pain—but she had to do something about getting some sleep. The head of a detective command couldn't function in that cloudy aftermath of daylight exhaustion. She required sustained bursts of energy and insight to do her job.

"It could be tension," suggested Fred Raphael, the dentist, who made room in his schedule late on Friday to put Maggie in the chair. He was engrossed in her mouth, tapping and magnifying the surfaces of her teeth. "Do you grind?"

"Not on a first date," she replied.

"There's been some grinding," he said solemnly. It was a reproach.

"Not by me. I swear to God."

"A lot of people do it without being aware. It's involuntary. We do it in our sleep."

"I didn't grind in my sleep."

"You wouldn't know if you're asleep, would you?"

"I don't sleep. That's my problem."

He was twisted over her shoulder, curling that angled mirror around her mouth. "You sleep. Maybe not as much as you'd like. But you sleep. I can see that some teeth do not quite mesh. Is this a time of unusual tension for you now?"

"Nothing I can do about that. I happen to have a high-stress job."

"You're lucky you're not a dentist."

"Right. Last-minute cancellations. Blatant teeth grinders in denial. I don't know how you do it."

He nodded, not even listening. He was absorbed in high dental speculation. "There are a lot of possibilities."

She gazed off at the print of Monet's garden in Giverny, which she could see through the treatment-room door on the wall of the waiting room. Under the print, someone was reading a magazine. Or seemed to be reading. The woman was furiously flipping the pages of one of the slick, oversized glamour publications and glaring with passionate resentment in Maggie's direction. This was a woman who blamed Maggie for eating into her appointment. And, Maggie guessed, this was a woman who was probably grinding her teeth.

"Temporomandibular joint dysfunction," Fred Raphael pronounced, pulling away, giving himself some authoritative distance, facing Maggie. His arms were folded across his chest and his expression was grave.

"Sounds bad," she said.

"No. Not really. Lots of ways to deal with it. First, let me attend to that cavity."

"What cavity?"

He sighed and gave her a sad, sorrowful look. "There's always a cavity."

Pudge Keene led the way to the food kitchen. He said that he knew of one in the neighborhood that was open on Friday evenings. The kitchen was operated out of St. James Episcopal Church at Seventy-first Street on Madison Avenue. He told the Man Murphy that he learned about it by calling a neighborhood coalition for the homeless. Lenox Hill Neighborhood Coalition, to be exact.

Murph knew instantly that it was a lie. There was something personal and embarrassing about Pudge's detailed and certain knowledge about the operation of the soup kitchen. Murph picked up that elusive and flickering component of a lie—the well-defined squeamish unease of the explanation. It was clearly untrue, but uttered in a way that committed the liar (Pudge) to his version. Of course, Pudge would not be able to back down; he'd just embellish and dig himself in deeper. Murph wanted to give it a pass, but he didn't know if he could.

They walked north along Lexington Avenue. It was cold and they were doing a fifteen-minute mile. They walked like old pros, scanning the shadows and the storefronts, checking out the foot traffic, watching each other's back. Not that there was anything to fear in this pampered part of town. What they were doing was nothing more than an exercise in two-man tactical police team foot mobility.

"So, my man, what kind of stuff do they have at this food kitchen?" asked Murph. It was a cruel question; he didn't mean to make the kid squirm, but he had Pudge in this tight little lie and he was curious; it was like catching a junkie with a pocket full of hundreds and getting some wild-ass tale of hitting a number or being on his way to pay off Grandma's hospital bill. Sometimes you hear this kind of lie coming at you like a freight train and you just stand there fascinated, watching it pick up steam, maybe pushing it along for the pure sadistic pleasure of seeing where it'll take you.

"You know, they have the usual crap—sandwich, soup, fruit, drink," replied Pudge.

"Uh-huh."

Pudge shot him a hard look. Now they both knew that they both knew.

"I just said, 'Uh-huh,'" said the Man Murphy, holding up his hands innocently.

But the temperature spiked between them, and wheels were

turning as they made their way uptown, and it became a twelve-minute mile. They hooked a left at Seventy-first Street, heading west past the fancy butchers and high-priced patisseries and small, dim bookstores, hitting the traffic lights just right. It was evening and they had to hurry. The food kitchens served early and Nafume could be in and out. The volunteers had to move a couple of shifts quickly in order to get home to their own dinners.

The two plainclothes cops lunged across Park Avenue, racing to the island so that they wouldn't be caught by a double dose of traffic. The church came up quickly, a red brick edifice with a large stained-glass window that would have looked at home in some New England square. It had a high pointy steeple and a neo-Gothic style.

Suddenly Pudge stopped and pulled Murph aside. "Look," he said, "I know this place." He hung his head, then shook off the hesitation. "I had an uncle, okay? He had a major drinking problem. This is my father's brother. Pissed away his life. And usually his paycheck. My aunt . . . well, let's just say that she was very needy. Every Friday night she sent my father out looking for him. Friday night, that was paycheck night. And she lived from hand to mouth. It was my job to go out with my father. It was a lousy job." Pudge sighed. "So, over the years, I've been to every shelter and Friday-night soup kitchen in the city, looking for my uncle. That's how I know about this place."

Murph put his hand on Pudge's shoulder and spoke in a low, sympathetic voice. "Ain't nothin', man," he said. "Everybody's got some shit in the closet. You know what bugs me: I am always afraid that someday I'm gonna bust some dime junkie and it turns out to be my old man."

Pudge looked pained.

"Course, that ain't ever gonna happen 'cause I have no idea what my old man looks like. Fact, I may have busted him already."

He smiled. Then Pudge smiled. They stood breathing steam for a moment, then turned back to the business at hand.

Outside the basement entrance to the kitchen was a line of

men. There were a few women, but both men and women had that same hollowed-out, spent look of defeat. They were all alike in their misfortune. Even the young looked old.

They waited in the cold, in muttering misery, for the meager meal of thin soup and a thick sandwich. There would be a piece of fruit—a gesture to appease the consciences of nutrition-minded volunteers. The well-meaning volunteers did what they could to deliver a complete, rounded meal. It was a thoughtful, generous thing. And yet the public garbage cans around the church spilled over with twice-rejected apples and oranges.

Pudge said he wanted permission first before they invaded the soup kitchen. They had to talk to whoever ran the operation. Murph wasn't about to argue. They climbed up the stairs to the church and made their way down the center aisle. In one of the pews there was a man cleaning up his bedroll. He was a shabby and thin derelict with a mountain-man beard and hands encrusted and cracked.

"Is there someone in charge of the soup kitchen?" asked Murph.

The man in the pew turned to them with blazing eyes. He seemed to rise higher on his feet. "Better seek a Bible!" he said in a voice that rang up to the balcony. No one else in the church took any notice. Apparently they were accustomed to such savage outbursts. "The good book: that's better food for the sinner!" cried the man in the pew.

Near the altar they saw an Episcopal priest talking to two women. They were parish women and they were leaning close to the priest in order to whisper, but the voices were loud enough to carry. The two plainclothesmen stood away, waiting their turn to talk to the priest, uncomfortably eavesdropping. Both women wore compact kerchiefs—they wore them like head bandages to protect their faces.

"He's not a bad boy, Father," said the one nearest the priest, her hands clutching the priest's. "You know, when he goes to school, he's very smart. The teachers all said that about him.

Could be . . . anything. That's what they said. Didn't they, Cissy?"

She turned to the other woman, who was too choked to speak; she merely nodded emphatically.

The priest was young and balding. He listened well, expectantly, yet with a scowling authority. He let the woman talk, drew her out. That priest would've made a good cop, thought Murph.

"It's the other boys," said the woman.

The priest rolled his eyes.

"Kevin's a follower," insisted the mother.

"Not having a father," said the second woman, and the mother seemed hurt by the remark. "It makes a difference to a boy," pressed the second woman, as much for the mother's benefit as for the priest. It was obviously an old bone of contention.

The priest turned to the mother. "Look, Margaret, face it, he does drugs," he said.

"Well," began the mother, Margaret, "he's had some problems, Father, I know that . . ."

"Margaret," the priest insisted, "they found the drugs on his person and in his room. You, yourself, found the bong. He's *known* to the police. He doesn't just take drugs. He sells them, for God's sake!"

The mother stammered. The aunt wept.

"I'll write the letter for you, Margaret; maybe it'll help. I doubt it. But I want him in some kind of program. The boy's an addict. Sooner or later he's going to kill himself or kill someone else. That's what they do."

This priest was streetwise and tough, thought Murph. A good man.

The women left and the priest turned to the two plainclothes policemen; he seemed a little annoyed that they had overheard the intimacies of his parishioners. But he also knew that they were cops. He knew it even before they flashed their shields. He was a man who knew all the blunt secrets around him. He introduced himself. Father Max Gross.

He listened to Pudge and the Man, respected the fact that

they came to him first, grasped the need, nodded, and led them to the basement soup kitchen. He even knew who they were looking for.

As they walked, Murph worried about the priest. He wondered when the crisis in faith would come. Not far off, he guessed. The priest wasn't yet forty, but the signs of fragile resignation and brittle resentment were starting to show like personality cracks. All that fine spiritual protective coating was wearing away.

"There," said the priest as they stood in the doorway of the hall; he nodded at a far table.

And there, at a table for four in the distant corner, where each of the men seemed a chronicle of human wreckage, sat Nafume Benjamin. When he looked up from his soup, Benjamin brightened at the sight of the two plainclothesmen.

"Familiar faces," said the priest, explaining the smile. "All these people," he added, looking around the sorrowful room, "they live in terrible isolation. You know, they're lonely." He nodded again in Benjamin's direction. "He's glad to see you."

Murphy thought, This priest is lonely, too.

FOURTEEN

The windows in room 315 of the Gotham Hotel leaked, there were no drapes to block the wind, and the steam heat was thin and unreliable. But Peggy O'Neill welcomed the wintry air. Mickey would last longer in a cold room.

"No sane person could do what I have done," she explained to Mickey.

How, then, did she interpret what she had done?

"I had no choice," she said mildly, addressing the stiffening corpse, along with an unseen jury. She was aware that there was no one listening except herself, and yet she found it a comfort to speak. "It was not my idea. They told me what to say. And then you told me what to do. You know me well enough to know that I would never do such things." She shook her head like a child. "Not on my own. Crushing a person's skull with a rock! And what happened to you! That's not me."

She nodded, satisfied with the explanations. And so, on the eve of one more stage of this unfolding tragedy, she discarded blame. It was all beyond her control. Peggy O'Neill was driven by the momentum of things that other people had started.

And in the dying hours of that Friday evening, another crucial factor came into play: Her life was over. This did not even frighten her. She accepted it. In fact, as she thought about it, Peggy had a hunch that from the beginning—from the moment she accepted the direction from the assistant in the greenroom to expand on her domestic grief and insert the false version of events into her tale—she was doomed.

On the set of *The Kevin Grant Show*, when the camera with the red light turned in her direction, in the airless, breathless, stitch of time, she grasped completely that nothing would ever be the same.

Of course now, as the hotel room grew darker and darker, as she began to appreciate that this thing had swung out of control and that she could never make it stop or go back to the beginning, she settled for one small consolation: She could control the conclusion. Once she accepted her own destruction, she had a grip on the outcome. On that point she was utterly unconfused.

"But that was your idea, too," she told Mickey.

Less than a week ago, her life was as ordinary and predictable as any other working-class survivor of a Catholic education. She obeyed the social expectations of hygiene (she bathed, brushed her teeth daily, and wore fresh clothing) and her public conduct was a model of modest rectitude (she excused herself when bumping into strangers, she acknowledged her friends with a sincere greeting, she smiled at appropriate moments and clucked when the occasion called for it). She functioned smoothly at work, she performed her duties without complaint—she anticipated, she provided, she supported . . .

And yet, sitting there in that bleak hotel room, on that broken chair, as the day ended, she understood that she was, in the end, emotionally maimed. For all that had taken place, for all that would take place, she felt . . . nothing. She never had. She had nothing but barren feelings for her dead ex-husband—not even hatred—nor for her exploitative boss nor for her needy and dull acquaintances. If she tried, she could conjure up a fuzzy memory of her parents, but no true sentiment. They were present in dreams, but some mystery kept them out of reach. She could not even remember the sounds of their voices, much less how she felt about them.

She behaved the way she did in order to satisfy the hopes of Mommy or Daddy or Micky or Mel. Or the producers of *The Kevin Grant Show.*

And so with a sigh of resignation, while staring at the flickering, snowy image on the television set, she began to prepare the final act. She placed a saucepan with an inch of water at the bottom on a portable burner. She emptied the digoxin tablets into the boiling water. The tablets soon melted into a mush. Then she reached into her large Bloomingdale's bag and removed the box of Godiva chocolates and the thin, scalpel-like razor. Carefully, as if she were an operating-room nurse, she set the hypodermic needle on the small, shaky hotel table. In the midst of her concentration, she looked over at Mickey and felt nothing.

He didn't understand. He thought that she was guilty of dirty secrets. Infidelity. He couldn't appreciate the true vice. Her real dirty secret was indifference. She cared for nothing and no one. The other great secret was competence. She was very good at things, which was, in a way, related to the indifference.

From time to time, she glanced up and looked at the television screen. It gave her eyes time to rest. This was taxing work, making tiny little holes in the bottom of each chocolate truffle, sucking out a portion of the filling with the needle, then replacing the center with the mush of digoxin, boiled down and combined with the water. Each truffle had at least five milligrams. The tricky part came when she had to seal the bottom of the truffle again so that there would be no trace of the tampering. Luckily the cold air kept the chocolates from losing their shape or melting.

She placed the pieces aside. It took her two hours to make five loaded truffles. But they looked delicious. She was almost tempted to taste one.

She picked up the phone and dialed Saks. She asked for customer service. She said that she was Judy Winner's new assistant and wanted to confirm tomorrow's appointment. There was a pause, then an assistant floor manager, then a floor manager got on the phone.

"Ms. Winner doesn't need an appointment," said the floor manager with some stiff pride. "Anytime is fine."

"I'm new," said Peggy. "I just want to make certain I don't screw up. Have to act like I know what I'm doing. What time does she usually come in?"

"Ten-thirty is her usual fitting," said the floor manager, with a boast of intimacy in disclosing her information.

Peggy hung up and began to hum quietly. One more truffle and she could sleep.

Peggy's mood brightened. Even the television gave Peggy's spirits a lift. The program playing on the broken set was a syndicated repeat of an old *Kevin Grant Show.* The theme was young girls who dressed like sluts. From what she could see through the haze of bad reception, the guests lived up to their billing. But when the camera closed in on the faces, she could tell, despite the poor quality of the picture, that the girls were children. They were children dressed up like sluts in a play written by Kevin Grant's producers.

"This may pinch."

Maggie rolled her eyes. Why did he have to say that? Because dentists were all empathetically dead. How else could they sink howling needles into soft gum tissue and call it a pinch? Sadists. Even Fred. Even the sweet, gentle, soft-spoken man who, at the moment, had his knuckles in her mouth, even he employed the same fiendish tactic before launching his dental blitzkrieg.

"The longer the shot takes, the more effective the Novocain," he said in that elevator-Muzak tone. Maggie felt like a fish with that steel needle loitering between her palate and her brain. Finally, he replaced the needle with rolls of cotton.

"Uh, hraph phaat skoon," she said through the barricade of cotton wads and an angled mirror and a steel pick.

"I will try," said Dr. Raphael.

"Kroggg!"

"Of course. Please rinse."

She had just enough time for a deep sigh before he began another attack on the doomed cavity.

It was not a pleasant thought, but Maggie had developed a qualm about Fred. During a recent cleaning, as he was chipping away at her implacable plaque with his miniature sledgehammer, he mentioned—merely as a conversational throwaway—that he was going on vacation. Somewhere in New England, he said. When Maggie asked what the hell he planned to do in New England in midwinter, he replied blandly that he was going to ski. As if that wasn't bad enough, he added matter-of-factly that he was a dedicated, lifelong downhill skier. Her opinion of the man never fully recovered.

"Kroot shooz bunnning urp?"

"I'm working as fast as I can," he said. She sensed a smile, but she couldn't really see it since Fred was masked like a bandit.

"Fllatt nooor Rammerrr! Ishht Aaark."

"Yes, I heard about that case. Poor woman. Is that yours?" He seemed to enjoy hearing about her work when he was supposed to be concentrating on the delicate task of fixing her teeth without causing unnecessary grief.

"Ah, chiiiit!"

"Sorry."

Whenever his drill struck an unmedicated nerve, Fred's apology was delivered in an infuriatingly mild tone. Before she got hold of the downhill image, she ascribed the lack of force in his contrition to a heightened sensitivity; he was a man who didn't want to excite her by making too much of a little bump against an exposed nerve. Now when he apologized, she heard someone who was only technically sorry.

"Lamm argh fooo!"

"I know you're in a hurry, Maggie, but if I didn't get to that cavity now it would have been much worse. We could lose the tooth."

He spoke of endangered teeth as if they were people in peril. She had an uncomfortable suspicion that he thought more of her teeth than he did of her.

"I had to get that cavity now. You know how you keep breaking appointments."

"Gruph niil wooor!"

"Your work is important. Of course. But you tend to come in only during an emergency. I have to grab you when I can."

And so he had gone to work with his needle and high-tech drill and bloody cotton rolls, and Maggie was left limp. Then, given who she was and what she did for a living, she had a terrible thought: Maybe there wasn't even a cavity. She shook the idea out of her mind. There was only a thin line between healthy suspicion and dangerous paranoia.

"About that jaw thingamajig," she said in her cotton-mouthed voice after he was done with the presumptive cavity.

"Ah, the TMJ," he said. "Well, you know, it could be tension. More common among women. It is a pain along the side of the face, in front of the ear."

Again, he looked inside her mouth.

"Did you bite down on something?"

She remembered now. In France a few weeks ago, Maggie and Jerry found themselves on the bullet train shooting south to Avignon, chasing her phantom killer. She sat across the aisle from a farmer. He was a huge man with a sack full of sandwiches. He laid them out on the fold-down table, then removed them from the bag with great care, one by one, turning them over and over, examining them like a tailor assessing a fine bolt of cloth. Then, when he was satisfied that the presentation was correct, the farmer with his thick, calloused hands removed the plastic wrap from them, again, one by one. Undressing a lover, she thought. There were eight sandwiches. It could have been lunch for a group, but it was the farmer's meal. They were eaten in sequence. He unfolded each wrapper carefully, without disturbing the contents, then smoothed the wrapper and used it as a plate. He placed each sandwich on top. He ate them slowly, with great appreciation and total concentration, as only a French farmer with ancient memories of the soil and an educated palate could do.

Maggie and Jerry had just come from Paris, where they had dined in three-star restaurants and had five-course meals; she had gotten drunk on exquisite wine and eaten herself beyond contentment with perfect gourmet food, but nothing had made her salivate like the sight of that old, fat farmer slowly unwrapping and eating his plain tomato sandwiches. He chewed with the lingering respect of a true food lover. She was embarrassed to watch.

Finally, she told Jerry that she had to get something to eat, although they were supposed to have a full sit-down dinner at a first-rate hotel in Avignon. Maggie made her way through the pitching train to the dining car, where she pointed to the picture display of a sandwich. She bit down on a hard, cold roll filled with tuna fish, and although her hunger was deflected, she felt the first ache of pain in her jaw. In spite of the pain she kept on eating. The soreness remained, coming alive at every meal and keeping her awake at night. But even now, telling Fred the story, the memory of the fat French farmer still made her hot for one of his sandwiches.

"You bit down on a sandwich." Fred Raphael nodded knowingly.

Maggie was roaming the inside of her mouth with her tongue, searching for feeling.

"That's pretty much what I do with a sandwich. I bite down on it."

"Well, that's what happened. Injured the joint. Now you should put a hot compress on the jaw," said the dentist. "That should ease the pain."

"What if it doesn't help?"

Fred Raphael shrugged. "There are the nonsteroidal anti-inflammatories. Advil. Nuprin. These things can go away overnight. Unless the bite is affected and the teeth don't mesh. But we have ways of helping with this."

She nodded. Okay, okay. God, how she hated the upkeep. Not even in her midthirties and already she was uploading way too many dental and health details. What was it gonna be like when she hit forty?

When her beeper went off she was still roaming around her gums with her tongue, feeling for more trouble. Pudge and Murph had Benjamin back at Manhattan North. But she wasn't ready to go yet.

"Listen, Fred, how hard is it to take out someone's teeth?"

He looked pensive for a moment. "You're too young," he replied. "True, you've had some problems, but nothing we can't handle. You wouldn't be happy with implants or dentures."

She laughed. "No. I mean, hypothetically, suppose you wanted to eliminate the possibility of tracing someone through dental records. Suppose you wanted to remove their teeth."

"The woman in the park," he said.

"Just suppose, goddamn it!"

He looked up at the ceiling. "Hard," he said. "Very hard. Unless you were a dentist." He laughed.

"Why hard?"

"Well, teeth are attached to the bone. You'd have to pull them, one by one. If the person was alive, she'd have to be sedated, she'd have to cooperate. If she was dead, the muscles would work against you. Sloppy."

"Couldn't you just smash them out?"

He shook his head.

"Too messy. Cracked bits all over the place. Unless, of course, she was wearing dentures. Then you just take them out."

Maggie smiled. Now she was ready. She almost ran out of the office to meet the plainclothesmen and Benjamin at the command post. On the way, she called in Sam. Get the coroner, she told him. Check the contents of the mouth of the corpse in the park. Find out if there was dental debris. Find out Peggy O'Neill's dental history. Call Mel Carr. See if she had dentures.

Maggie didn't even feel the ache in her jaw.

FIFTEEN

What was that? It sounded like a squeak. Maybe a peep. A little peep squeak. Definitely not a grunt.

Chief of Detectives Larry Scott, who was out of uniform and sweating from every pore of his body while hovering on the brink of a pretty convulsive orgasm, lowered his frowning face closer to the naked woman writhing underneath him, and inquired, "What the hell was that?" He managed to continue the primary action in spite of this strange digression.

Nora Romano, the woman who was going along hand in hand, sharing the chief's erotic commotion, had arrived at her own late stage of ardor and was thus highly annoyed by the inopportune question. She opened her clenched eyes and had an expression which was a combination of exasperation and wonder.

"What?" she gasped.

Persevering—slipping and sliding—Chief Scott managed to query again through clenched teeth and rapid breaths.

"I said, 'What the hell was that noise?' "

"Noise?"

Nora Romano, who was the civilian assistant to Marty Klein in the police department's public-relations office, misunderstood the question and jumped in alarm. She attempted to pull away from the chief because, in spite of the urgency of the present situation, she greatly feared discovery of this ethically compromising and hopelessly incorrect—from a political and social standpoint—tryst. If they were discovered, not only would it cost her an enviable job and blemish her future career possibilities, but it would forever diminish her rank among her ultra-sensitive and snobby social friends. Ivy League girls did not sleep with cops, unless, of course, they were culturally slumming. "You heard a noise?" she asked.

"Well, not so much a noise," puffed Chief Scott, gripping Nora's shoulders tightly in case she tried to pull away again. "But it, uh, wasn't a grunt. Whenever we do it, you always grunt."

He was disappointed that she flubbed the animal noise! Now that she understood the nature of the digression, Nora regained some of the lusty warmth she first felt when she popped open her dress and flung herself wantonly on the bed of her Chelsea apartment for what the chief routinely called "a quickie"—a term which ordinarily would have irritated her feminist sensibilities, but which had the perverse opposite effect of cloaking the whole project with an air of sin.

The chief—which was how she thought of him—enjoyed the animal grunt. A lot, judging by his bug-eyed excitement and zest as she wiggled and squirmed like a slippery fish. The chief read Nora's increased activity as reciprocal passion. He began to wheeze and moan—the prelude to his grand finale. The heightened commitment was contagious and boosted Nora's level of enthusiasm.

Now that this bizarre wrinkle of grunting had been introduced to their sexual repertoire, Nora felt a thrilling new dimension of power and interest. The man responded to pure basic sounds. Like a whale.

Not that she felt any personal affection for the chief. All in all, viewed objectively, he was repulsive. He was a married man, a pompous career climber, a sexist pig and, worst of all, he had a bad body odor. She suspected far more grave character flaws. However, Nora knew that she was no bargain herself. She was a thirty-two-year-old woman with a slight weight problem and a habit of personal hysteria that drove her lovers fleeing into the total avoidance protection program. The pattern was always the same: After three or four intense encounters—following an exposure to her excessive demands, loud objections, nitpicky grievances—they all simply vanished. It had been a year since her last affair, and she settled for these clandestine late-Friday encounters with the chief out of sheer physical desperation.

Although she hated to admit it, sex with this odious savage was fun. And she realized—now that she thought about it—that he was right; she had intentionally withheld her grunts. Why? Because she secretly knew that he liked the grunts; and she had a reason for punishing him. It was a little payback for something he said while they were out of their minds with heat. A remark. She explained this to the chief as best she could between little sobs as she progressed in her animal momentum and overall enthusiasm: "You . . . called me Maggie."

Unable to comprehend or decelerate, the chief replied, as best he could, "I . . . *Oh!* . . . did not . . . *Oh, God!* . . . call you, *Oh, dear God!* . . . Maggie!"

"Yes, *uh, uh, uh,* you did!"

They peaked together in the middle of this bickering side issue about grunting and Maggie. Then they fell back on the bed, surrounded by Nora's stuffed dolls and lace pillows.

"That was great!" sighed the chief in his infuriatingly contented manner.

Nora lifted herself on an elbow. "You are obsessed with her, you know," she said.

"Who?"

"Lieutenant Van Zandt."

"Listen, Babe, I did not call you Maggie. I would remember."

"You called me Maggie."

"Never. You misunderstood."

"How could I misunderstand that? You called me by another woman's name!"

"Maybe I said, 'Don't nag me!' "

Nora looked at him. She hadn't fully grasped it before—in fact, she would have thought it unlikely, given his particular job—but the man was a liar. Then she thought, I will have to take this into consideration when dealing with the press.

At that instant, they heard a noise. Neither a grunt nor a squeak. A little tinkle. They both looked around, as if some third party were hiding somewhere in the room. Then the sound began again—a buzzing sound—and they both realized what it was and reached around the bed for their respective briefcases, inside which were their respective cellular phones. The one that was ringing was inside Chief Scott's attaché case.

"Would you mind waiting in the bathroom?" he said, before punching the power button. "This could be a security thing."

"This is my apartment!"

He simply looked at her with a disapproving frown.

She went into the bathroom muttering and cursing, holding the bedsheet tightly around her shoulders, vowing to end this thing now, once and for all because: First of all, he was married, second she was better than he was, third he was a liar, fourth he had this thing for Maggie, fifth it wasn't even great sex . . . well, it was sex and, in fact, she enjoyed this new grunting thing. . . .

The call was from Chief Scott's aide, Sergeant Gil Player.

"Sorry," began Player.

"What's up?" asked the chief, who was feeling a surge of potency now that he detected Nora's jealousy.

"There's a thing," said the sergeant. "Maggie."

"You, too?"

"What?"

"Never mind. What about Maggie?"

"She's really working this park thing. Got everybody in the

task force humping. Friday night. You know how that pisses people off."

"Yeah, so?"

"Well, she's trying to prove that body in the park wasn't the TV lady."

There was a heartbeat of silence. Then Chief Scott said, "How? I mean, who knows who the fuck that body was? I mean, that cadaver had been to a chop shop. How the fuck . . . C'mon! I mean, that fuckin' Maggie! Shit. Damn!"

He had issued the deep backgrounder, confiding to picked reporters that the woman in the park had probably been killed by her husband; that it was coincidence that she appeared on a talk show.

It would have been simpler if the body was Peggy O'Neill. Dead. Gone. Search for the husband. Take the heat off of Kevin Grant. Now there would be more probing. More annoying questions without sufficient answers. It would keep the story alive. Revive the Kevin Grant connection. Make the mayor mad.

"Maggie!" he muttered.

Through the crack in the bathroom door, Nora Romano listened to the chief's side of the conversation. Maggie! That woman was getting on Nora's nerves, too.

At that moment, on Manhattan's Upper East Side, Maggie and Officers Pudge Keene and the Man Murph, along with the shabby Private Benjamin, walked down the steps and into Serendipity, a kind of upscale ice-cream parlor and hamburger shop. Maggie thought Benjamin would talk easier in a civilian setting.

There was an intake of shock from the young, clean-cut customers and staff. Maggie, Pudge, Murph, and Benjamin marched past the manager and grabbed an empty table in the back.

"It's reserved," said the manager, running to catch up with Maggie, who was leading the charge.

The restaurant was almost empty. It was too late for the pre-movie crowd and too early for the posttheater rush.

"We're not going to steal the table," said Maggie, showing the manager her gold detective lieutenant's shield.

"Please," whispered the manager into Maggie's ear.

"We'll only be a minute," replied Maggie, trying to pacify the man. She was mild and understanding. After all, he had his business to attend to. "Really, we'll only be a few minutes. I promise."

"But the table really is reserved," insisted the manager. He was a tall man who was on the far side of forty—a former golden youth, she suspected, from the thinning blond surfer hair, the chic silk shirt with all the buttons smartly buttoned to the collar, and the expensive beige linen jacket—the kind of fringe social gigolo who stood sentry for his betters. "I can't help you," he said.

Maggie's first instinct was always to try to be reasonable. Sometimes, however, people misconstrued her conciliatory style as weakness. Sometimes they tried to push her.

"Reserved, huh?" asked Maggie, looking around at the empty tables, front to back.

"Afraid so," said the manager, lulled into thinking that he had a winning tactic. "Holding it for a steady customer."

"Okay, so we'll move over there," said Maggie, pointing to another table close to the kitchen.

The manager looked at the table. "I'm afraid that one is taken, too."

"I'll bet that they're all taken," said Maggie agreeably, nodding, surveying the empty room.

"Pretty much." The manager smiled, as if he'd hammered out an understanding.

Maggie motioned the manager down with her index finger. When he bent over she said, in a voice that carried, "Then I'm gonna hafta commandeer this table. Police business."

"What? Are you serious?"

"I am," said Maggie mildly. "I have the power, you know."

He looked shocked.

"And, unless I get some service, someone will hafta answer to a charge of obstruction," said Maggie, still smiling.

The manager nodded dumbly and motioned over a waiter.

"Cappuccino," said Maggie. The waiter, a college kid who depended on tips for tuition, sensed a wasted night.

"There's a minimum," he said.

Maggie laughed. "Okay," she said. "Throw in four hamburgers, four orders of french fries, four hot dogs, four large Cokes, and four supersundaes."

"What flavor?" asked the surprised waiter.

Maggie paused a beat, allowing the heat of her impatience to radiate over to the waiter. "Surprise us," she replied.

"You are one wild date," said Murph.

"You know, I wish I had you with me at Burger King," said Benjamin. "They won't serve me."

"We're working," said Maggie, in that same hard occupational tone of voice.

"You know, I just ate," said Benjamin, "but I believe that I could handle an after-dinner snack."

"I missed dinner," said Murph.

"Me, too," added Pudge.

"Yeah, well I got dental aftermath," said Maggie. "You guys can split mine."

The food came quickly, hastened by the urgent command of the manager. He wanted this table cleared quickly. It worked as Maggie had suspected—they could talk in peace, no one sat near them.

"Tell me again what happened," said Maggie, sipping delicately at the cappuccino. "When you found the purse."

Benjamin's mouth was full of potatoes and ground beef. He took his time washing down the food with the huge soda. "I was digging around the garbage," he said, "looking for cans."

Maggie shook her head.

"What was I doin', if I wasn't lookin' for cans?"

"You weren't looking for cans. Not on a cold night in January when people are drinking out of nonrefundable paper cups."

Pudge and Murph had not seen the point—until now. She was guessing at something. But it was good guessing.

"That's what I was doin'," insisted Benjamin.

She sighed and bent closer, talking intimately. "Look, Nafume, I'm not out to break your chops. Didn't I wine and dine you on fancy food?"

"Actually, I prefer takeout," he said. "At least you can smoke when you're eating takeout."

"Tell me what happened." There was no give in her voice.

The rag man pushed the hood away from his face. He looked worried. Then he said quickly, "Yeah, yeah, I saw the lady throw the bag away."

Maggie leaned closer. "What lady?"

"The lady who came out of the park. She wore this dumpy hat. I saw her come up to the can and throw the bag away. I thought she was a dip, you know? Snatched the bag and then tossed it. Looking around. Checking to make sure no one sees her. And no one did. Just me."

"But she wasn't. A purse snatcher."

"No. She was straight."

"Did she look like this?"

Maggie slapped a photograph of Peggy O'Neill on the table. The rag man took his time before he looked. Then, slowly, he said, "Could be. Hard to tell without seein' her in the hat."

Maggie remembered Mel Carr telling her that Peggy O'Neill always wore a dumpy hat.

"Why didn't you tell me before?" asked Maggie finally.

Nafume was picking off french fries from her plate. "I didn't know the legal implications," he said.

"You thought we'd bust you for theft?"

He shrugged. "I don't know what I thought. The law of the street, lady. Don't volunteer shit."

They finished the meal in silence.

SIXTEEN

SATURDAY, JANUARY 14

It was a few minutes after seven in the morning and the cold rain tapped against the large restaurant window on Greenwich Street in lower Manhattan. Inside the Village Den, Maggie and Jerry were both in that fuzzy aftermath of sleepless bliss, sipping scalding coffee and waiting for breakfast. Maggie smiled, remembering the high-pitched physical pleasure of the night before. And then she looked across the table and noticed Jerry Munk preening with smug male pride.

"Pretty good," he said, mistaking her astonished reaction for performance appreciation.

Maggie paused, surprised at Jerry's raw vanity. "Nah," she said coolly, "not so good. As a matter of fact, I happen to prefer mine a little stronger."

Jerry's eyes widened. "Stronger?" he asked, sitting up straighter. "Really?"

"You have to admit, it's a little weak," she said, looking down at the mug of coffee. He followed her eyes, then laughed.

The waitress arrived with Maggie's plate of fried eggs, home fried potatoes, a double order of bacon, and well-buttered toast. Jerry, who had half a grapefruit and dry toast, was overcome by the odor of Maggie's meal.

"You know," he said with paternal sarcasm, "I'm getting a lot of secondhand cholesterol just sitting here. You'd think that they'd have a low-fat section."

"I'll try to get rid of it as soon as possible," said Maggie, ravenously digging into the meal.

He shook his head and dipped carefully into the squirting grapefruit.

The restaurant was sprinkled with the usual Saturday-morning mix of postjogging zealots, demanding children taking advantage of weekend fathers, hangdog leftover fish from all-night revels, and the obligatory brooding artist, distanced from the rest of the universe by a dark nimbus of creative suffering. The soft murmurings of subdued conversation drifted through the room like a soothing mist.

Maggie and Jerry felt a cozy sensation of safe, familiar acceptance within the heated dining room. Suddenly, they were awakened from their dreamy state by a frigid blast of wind as the door opened and Detective Sergeant Sad Sam Rosen stood for a moment, shaking off the cold, searching for Maggie. Heads turned in silent reproach as Sam stood in the doorway. Then he noticed Maggie's hand raised in greeting and nodded.

"Coffee," said Sam to the waitress as he slid into the booth beside Jerry; he pointed to Maggie's plate of eggs and potatoes and bacon and toast. "I'll have the same."

"You guys!" said Jerry. "Sugar, butter, greasy food. I'm surprised you don't smoke."

Maggie and Sam exchanged a glancing, knowing look of recognition. "It's a cop thing," she explained.

"Cold," said Sam, slapping his hands together. He wrapped them around the mug when the waitress brought the coffee. Maggie noticed that he was scanning the room, checking for eavesdroppers. She could tell this was a heightened state of alert.

"Took the subway," said Sam, still delaying his purpose. Maggie was patient. "Kid ahead of me jumped the turnstile and some undercover cop nailed him. So the kid gets sick to his stomach and starts throwing up. You know, projectile vomit. Everybody groans and looks away. The cop, too, takes one disgusted look and walks away from the arrest."

Maggie and Sam laughed. Cop thing, thought Jerry.

"Subways!" said Sam, devouring a piece of toast offered by Maggie.

The waitress with the slouch of weary occupational gloom laid down Sam's plate of food. He was hungry and he attacked his food with enthusiasm.

"I had a subway thing . . . last week," began Maggie. "I was on a Lex—didn't wanna hit traffic and my squad car was already uptown—and I'm only thinking about a meeting with Scottnose, not paying much attention to the surroundings, just enduring the uptown train. So halfway there I notice this guy getting a little too sociable, you know? He's rubbing against me like a cat. Nasty, vile-looking creep. Now, I'm not interested in busting some skanky thrill-seeker—I got a big meeting uptown and I'm late. I start thinking about the arrest, the paperwork, the court time. The meeting. So I used the old finger."

Sam nodded, his head buried in the food.

"What's that?" asked Jerry, nibbling at his dry toast. "What's the old finger?"

Maggie grabbed a large last slice of bacon. "I put my finger up my nose," she said easily, while still chewing on the bacon. "Up to the knuckle."

Jerry lost his appetite. "You picked your nose?"

She nodded. "Of course. Works every time. Degenerates, boosters, muggers, scags—no one wants to go up against the dirty digit."

"Especially if you hit pay dirt," added Sam, wolfing down a spillover forkful of potato and loose eggs.

"Cop thing," said Maggie, seeing the horrified expression on Jerry's face.

"Hey! You're not eating," said Sam.

Jerry was looking up at the ceiling. "It's a delicate, New Age temperamental thing," he said.

"Three checks?" asked the waitress, who couldn't pick out the captain at this particular table.

"I'll take it," said Maggie, holding out her hand.

They were finished with the food, and the waitress left the plates behind—a visible reminder that their main business was done and they should be moving along.

"So, let me guess why you phoned," said Maggie, forcing Sam to explain the reason for his urgent call and clandestine meeting. "The chief wants to give me more people, boost my authority, and let me run my own investigation. Is that about right?"

Sam looked at Jerry. He wasn't sure he should be talking shop—not this high-level policy kind of shop—with someone outside of the police family. Maggie recognized the reluctance and saw that as the first sign of real trouble.

"Jerry's cool," she said, smiling. "Maybe not in the trendsetting style sense, but in the loyal-friend meaning of the term."

Sam shrugged.

"I'm goin' for a walk," said Jerry, forcing Sam to let him out of the booth. Maggie didn't try to stop him.

"Remember the digit defense," she called after him.

"I'll be up at the store," he said. "Thanks for a lovely weekend."

Maggie knew that Between the Covers—his bookstore on the Upper East Side—wasn't supposed to open for two and a half hours, and that Jerry would probably get up there early, lock himself inside the shop, and start reading one of his own tomes, spilling coffee on the pages and dog-earing his place so he could never sell it. He would never complain or resent her higher professional priority, and she felt a pang, a true silent tribute of grateful affection for the man. It was a version of deep respect, and she thought that maybe it outranked the other strong emotions she felt for Jerry Munk.

"Nice guy," remarked Sam, who, as Maggie's chief aide, ranged comfortably in her emotional slipstream. Although slower to declare himself, Sam was a reliable check of her judgment.

Of course, she knew another side to Jerry. There was a moment in Paris when he refused to budge. They had been racing from town to town, looking for elusive clues in her obsessive murder case, and now she wanted to cancel a dinner date and head for Avignon a day early.

"Listen," he had said, "I'm not against catching killers. I'm not even opposed to rearranging schedules and skipping meals. But I have looked forward to this dinner. La Coupole. I'm tired. No!"

"You're pissing in my lake," she said.

It was a new reference. His lifelong operating theosophy, he said. Based on a joke. They were standing on a footbridge over the Seine when he delivered it. "It's about writers and editors. The world is divided between writers and editors. . . ."

"I get it. I get it. Wisdom. Philosphy. A joke."

"A writer and an editor are walking in the woods and they come upon a beautiful, pristine lake. They both agree that it's perfect. Suddenly, the editor unzips his pants and starts to piss in the lake. The writer is horrified. 'What the hell are you doing?' he asks.

"The editor replies, 'Making it better.' "

She thought about it for a while. "That's your philosophy?"

"I don't think people should piss in someone else's lake."

"I'll be happy if you leave the seat down," she replied.

That was a month ago. Now, as she sat in a restaurant on Greenwich Street and watched Jerry Munk vanish into the subway, Maggie agreed with Sam.

"Soooo," she said, turning away from the window, "what's up?"

He avoided her eyes. This was painful for him. She could see it in the wide and perplexed swing of his head, usually so still and watchful.

"Scott's taking the case away from you," he said with the flat voice of an old cop delivering bad news.

Still, Maggie didn't quite grasp Sam's meaning. "What case? Manny Stern?" she asked, referring to the dead lawyer and his wife. That was the case that she had hunted beyond the boundaries of regulations and all common sense. That was the case upon which she spent her own money—something that was not forgivable to the old-time expense account chiselers.

"No, not the Sterns," said Sam.

She felt the beginning of anger.

"Last night, they had a big thing at the fortress," said Sam. "All the chiefs." He smiled thinly, knowing that they both instantly conjured up identical images of that suffocating conference room with scowling superchief faces and ratlike scampering as they shifted responsibility, ducked blame, wisecracked about absent colleagues, and came away with the names of scapegoats.

"And Scott sold me out," she announced, as if it were she, not Sam, delivering the news.

"Your name came up. Someone had to feed the press the story about the lady in the park and the talk-show lady. Apparently it was you."

She stopped him.

"It was Scott," she said. "He gave the backgrounder."

"Of course."

"You know, I don't like getting yanked. Not that this case is so charming. But I know how to go after it. I know the body ain't the lady on the talk show. I got that eyewitness saying she put her own handbag in the garbage. It bugs me. I think about it. You think that Scott thinks about it? I don't think so. I wonder, What's goin' on? Is her ex running Peggy O'Neill? Is she a hostage? You know that Scott isn't going to chase this one like me."

"No."

"So, I'm not gonna let it happen," Maggie said finally.

"You know why? Because I'm not ready to be pulled off the case."

"Really? How are you gonna stop it?"

She ran her hand through her thick mane of hair. "I'm not sure yet."

Dr. Judy Winner heard the sad music all night long. She pretended to sleep—she needed her rest—but she couldn't. What kept her awake was the vision of Kevin, sitting in the living room under the twenty-foot-high ceiling, with his feet propped up on the teakwood coffee table, drinking imported beer, maybe some Chivas Regal whiskey, while playing old Hank Williams ballads.

She heard the sorrowful words of the cowboy songs as she lay there in her own separate bedroom, her eyes clenched shut in case he came in to see if she was asleep.

She wondered if the other tenants at the Dakota heard the music. The walls were thick enough to preserve the peace; this was not the usual overpriced luxury building where the tenants were separated by thin plywood borders. This was the Dakota, the crown of American urban splendor, built by nineteenth-century capitalists to mimic French country grandeur. In spite of the fact that there were taller buildings around it, the Dakota loomed over the Upper West Side neighborhood.

The residents were the carefully chosen cream of America's aristocracy—tycoons, artists, famous actors, important journalists, old-money socialites. They lived in plush suites of ten or more rooms. There were roof gardens and private sanctuaries and wrought-iron elevators run by men with white gloves.

True, there were nouveau celebrities who gate-crashed their way in by virtue of prodigious wealth or cultural curiosity. But they soon disgraced themselves with too much sex, too many drugs, too much greed. They were not the durable and amusing eccentrics who wandered the cellars naked, or kept stuffed horses in full armor in their entryways.

An occasional scandal never seemed to affect the pleasant elevator greetings.

In the morning Dr. Judy showered and still heard the music

over the torrent of water. She heard it over the blast of the hair dryer. And her hand was not quite steady when she applied her eyeshadow and liner and lipstick. There was the appointment at Saks to keep; for a moment she considered canceling it, but then she thought that might make things worse. She could, as a good psychologist, find behavioral reasons to justify her shopping trip, to do the things she wanted to do. Just now it was her job to minimize her husband's problem, to put the disappearance of the talk-show guest into a rational perspective. What good would it do to join her husband in his self-pitying and pointless funk? Besides, she had made a different bargain. She thought that she was getting a man who would be a smooth escort through life. No bad habits. No complicated past entanglements. No unpleasant demands.

"You have plans for today?" she asked, pausing at the living-room entryway. The Klee above the couch, she noticed, was slightly off center. She must speak to the new maid.

"Plans?"

Kevin Grant's face was riddled with sorrow. The all-night drinking had driven deep canals into his cheeks.

"Are you going to do something? Do you want to meet for lunch? No, I have an appointment for lunch. Bill. He's trying to get me a syndicated column. Not that I want to take on any more. But, well, I have to talk to him about it."

He looked bewildered. "You really think . . . ? I mean . . ."

His body shrank. He had a moment of puffed hope, seeing her there in the doorway, pulling on her gloves, smelling of perfume, undaunted by the prospect of sensation, making optimistic plans. But then he realized that no matter what happened to him, Judy would not suffer ignominy. She would bear up bravely, speak of it sensibly, survive heroically. The hardships and burdens were his alone.

"Don't do this," she said briskly, a moral authority delivering instructions. "This is not productive. You have nothing to apologize for. We'll talk about it later. I'll call."

Well, it was his fault. He knew what he was doing. And he shook his head slowly and felt the wind of the door as she left, on her way to Saks.

The cab dropped her off at the corner of Forty-ninth Street and Fifth. She paid, calculating the 15-percent tip. The rain had stopped, but it was still cold. Pedestrians walked at an aerobic rate to get out of the weather. January in New York.

She didn't notice the woman in the brown coat watching her from the entrance to Saks. The woman pulled a tray out from under her coat, emptied out a bag of candy onto the tray, arranged the candy in succulent rows, then moved out into the center of the street.

Dr. Judy was thinking about a vacation. In France. Of course, there could be complications. The police might want Kevin close to help in the investigation.

The thought of greater, darker implications did not enter her mind. She had her own image and her career to think about.

She was in a state of muddled absorption, sorting out which problems were hers and which belonged to Kevin—almost like working out a settlement. From the corner of her eye she noticed the woman in the brown coat handing out chocolates. She had a sign that said *Godiva*. The brown outfit and the tray gave the woman street-corner authenticity.

Dr. Judy knew better than to indulge in a fat- and sugar-laden snack, but she couldn't resist the temptation. It was, she told herself, a legitimate consolation. A woman ahead of her, also about to enter Saks, took a piece, nibbled, and paused. "Very unusual taste," said the woman thoughtfully.

"New item," explained the lady in the brown coat. The first woman nodded and swallowed the rest of the chocolate, reassured that she was taking part in a street test-marketing strategy.

"New item," said the woman in the brown coat holding the Godiva tray; Dr. Judy smiled. She could use a new item. She reached over and took a large, walnut-sized piece of chocolate off the tray. She did not think that it was risky to eat food served from strangers in the street. She thought, in that meager portion of her attention devoted to the act, that she was getting something for nothing. She took it the way she took an hors d'oeuvre at a cocktail party—without a second thought.

The taste struck her as bittersweet as she swallowed the candy, but something else was more unsettling. As she took the candy and placed it whole in her mouth, she thought that she recognized the face of the woman in the brown coat. She was so focused on remembering where she had seen the woman, placing the woman's face, that she didn't pay attention to the tang of digoxin and the heightened pace and power of her heart rate. She felt a sudden, almost immediate, dizziness, and saw a flareup of colors—vivid greens and blinding yellows—as she wobbled through the door of Saks Fifth Avenue and steadied herself against a counter.

SEVENTEEN

Hector Bonilla was paying a kind of twilight attention to his job. The young security guard stationed at the north entrance of Saks Fifth Avenue was daydreaming about the benefits of working a weekend shift while defending the entryway against the street-corner panhandlers who reeked of urine and tried periodically to sneak in out of the cold.

He wasn't concerned about the Godiva lady handing out free chocolates; he was amused at the elegant ladies in fancy furs taking great gobs of candy from her tray. The men passing by didn't seem interested. They probably felt, as he did, that there was something a little undignified—maybe even a little unmanly—about accepting free candy; too much like admitting a weakness.

But then he thought about the woman giving away candy, placing it within his professional orbit, and decided that he might have an occupational concern. Hector's duty was as a sentry, charged with maintaining order at his post, but did it extend out into the street? He wasn't clear. Was the woman allowed to block the entrance? He didn't know. Did she have approval? He made a mental note to check.

With relief he saw that the Godiva lady was gone when he

looked out again. He was thus spared another embarrassing session with his supervisor, who seemed to delight in belittling him. Every time he had a question, it presented another opportunity for the supervisor to point out the vast limitations and ignorance of the new security guard.

Hector had just returned from smoking a cigarette in the back alley; he was envisioning a long lunch hour, which, on a Saturday, was a pleasant thing to contemplate. He wouldn't have to fight the hordes of white-collar office geeks for a spot at the counter of Hamburger Heaven, and he could flirt openly with Maria, the perky waitress who never charged him for his beverage or for his dessert.

He was perplexed about the wedding ring Maria wore; he didn't know whether it meant that she was married or just fending off a lot of annoying advances. He guessed the latter because she didn't seem the type to cheat, although nowadays, after the things he had seen in his new job as a security guard, he would not swear for anyone's integrity: Rich ladies caught flagrantly shoplifting underwear lamely insisted that it was a simple oversight.

In that half-alert, half-drowsy state, facing out into the street, Hector heard and felt something urgent behind him. When he turned he found a breathless woman in mink who smelled of expensive perfume pulling at his sleeve. He was about to say something sharp, because he didn't want to ruin the drape of his new gray sport jacket, but then he was struck by the apparent alarm on her face and he further noticed the excited flurry of activity at the other end of the store—customers and floor managers and salespeople were all rushing in the direction of the east escalator.

The woman in the mink coat kept tugging his sleeve and pointing to the epicenter of the commotion.

Nodding, Hector left his post and elbowed his way through the crowd that clotted around the escalator. When he cleared a path, he saw that someone had fallen and was lying on the first step of the up escalator. It was a customer, a woman, and her head kept banging again and again against the still-churning escalator stairs. Her coat and dress had ridden up high during the fall, exposing the raw flesh of her thighs. Her twitching legs were splayed out and onto the main floor. Hector's first impulse was to turn away from the woman's naked vulnerability. However, he reminded himself that he had a duty, he was there to assist. Hector held up a hand to keep everyone back and barked into his small radio transmitter.

"Get an ambulance!" he ordered the supervisor in the eighth-floor security room. "Call nine-one-one!"

"What's going on?" asked the supervisor in the command post.

"Woman down on one," he replied, remembering the procedure. "At the up escalator. Probably a coronary. I could use some help down here."

"On the way!" He heard the onset of panic in the supervisor's voice and it left him oddly pleased; for the first time he felt that he had the upper hand.

Meanwhile, another security guard appeared and Hector took command. He ordered the second guard to keep the crowd away from the woman—give her breathing room—then deputized the nervous floor manager to organize the sales help to form a human cordon around the area and to urge the customers to back away. He also ordered the floor manager to find someone to stand at his empty post on the door—he didn't want the store looted during the crisis. Then he reached over and hit the emergency stop switch, shutting down the escalator. The whining sound of the dying motor left a deep silence in the large first-floor cove, which smelled of wood polish and flowers.

Finally, Hector bent over and gently pulled the woman's head away from the hard metal stairs of the escalator. He moved her away carefully to a prepared spot and laid her head on her large shoulder bag. The bag was as big and soft as a pillow. He noticed that she was a middle-aged, heavyset woman and that she was foaming at the mouth. Her eyes were wide with fear, and that was a good sign. It meant that she was still alive.

Just then he heard the distant wail of approaching sirens, and at the same time he saw a swarm of grim, uniformed New York City police officers coming at him. They walked quickly down the aisles, as if they would crash through anything that got in their path. They came through the makeup department, past the perfume counters, brushing aside the pretty mannequins still frozen with the free spray bottles of cologne in their achingly thin hands. Hector was impressed by the speed and clean efficiency of the police. They maneuvered with comforting and resolute authority. They didn't waste time or effort as they approached from all points of the compass. They sealed off the area neatly; one of them even grabbed a large standing sign advertising a postholiday sale, improvising a screen by placing it between the onlookers and the lady on the ground. A trained and competent force, he thought.

An emergency medical service team was right behind the police, and they went to work on the stricken woman. While one EMS woman bent to take vital signs, another opened the victim's coat, unbuttoned a tight blouse, and made certain that the neck was clear for breathing. There was a minimum amount of talking—just the curt, businesslike chatter of professionals on a mission.

"I'm not getting a pulse . . .," said an EMS technician with a stethoscope pressed to the downed woman's neck.

"Open a line for me," ordered the senior EMS technician, and another nodded, cut up the woman's silk blouse, and cleaned off a vein before plunging a needle into the woman's arm.

A second ambulance had responded and a third technician put an oxygen mask over the woman's face, then pounded down on her chest. Hector watched the woman's body tremble from the blow, but he did not see any spontaneous movement from her. The blows came quickly and the body arched up and then collapsed into its own empty sack.

"Get the paddles," ordered the senior technician.

The junior technician looked up from his pressure point. "Still no signs." Another technician carrying a red case ran toward them, but it was too late for the paddles.

"Let's move her," said the senior man finally, with a resigned tone.

Behind him, Hector heard a sob, then someone uttered, "Dear God," and finally there was a high, dainty squeal of grief. Not a cry, just some elemental sound, a lament for a fellow fallen creature. Finally, as they lifted the woman onto the stretcher, he heard someone in the dense crowd say in a tone of absolute certainty, "She's dead!" And he knew, as everyone knew, that it was true. It was as if a priest had delivered the last rites.

In all, the whole episode had taken six minutes. That was the total elapsed time since the woman in mink tugged at his sleeve to alert him to the emergency to the final recognition of extinction. Life had come and gone that quickly. It was a sobering and frightening thing to contemplate. All the modern technology was useless. He felt safe at Saks Fifth Avenue, but it was an illusion.

As the EMS crew began wheeling out the dead woman, everyone from store manager to casual shopper stood in awed silence at the shock of mortality.

Then, in the midst of the pause and contemplation on the suddenness of death, there came a cry from the top of the escalator stairs: "Hey! Hey!"

A supervising police sergeant looked up. He was handling the routine with breezy professionalism. He had already instructed his uniformed officers to take the names of witnesses, to go through the victim's purse for ID, to find out if she was alone or with someone, and to find someone to notify; he was attending, in short, to the necessary bureaucratic details of one more amendment in the daily turnover of the census of a great city, when the shout came down from above.

"Third floor! Third floor!" came the urgent voice.

"What's going on?" replied the sergeant in the commanding voice he used to break open bolted doors.

"Get an ambulance! A woman! She collapsed!"

Maggie was made to sit outside Chief Scott's office at One Police Plaza for half an hour before he finally summoned her inside. She entered quietly and settled into the brown leather chair opposite his desk, waiting to hear the news she already knew. The chief was bent over a case file. He turned the pages slowly, never looking up, never speaking, never acknowledging her presence.

Maggie was aware of an excess amount of acid in her stomach, which she attributed not to the chief's malicious display of power, but rather to the second order of bacon.

To distract herself, she looked around at the walls. They were crowded with photographs—all of which had the young and middle-aged face of Larry Scott in the same tense, death-mask smile. The Larry Scott memorial walls, she thought. There was Chief Scott looking stiff as he stood alongside politicians, the usual gang of visiting movie actors, and community and religious leaders.

On another section of a wall there was a long chain of group pictures of various assembled police units and commands from which it was possible to chart the steady advance in Larry Scott's career, as he moved from the fringes to the centers of the photographs.

Nowhere was there a picture of his wife and children.

But then he broke her mood by lifting his head.

"I want you to run over to Saks," he said.

She thought that she detected sarcasm. Her back began to stiffen.

"There's something going on there—a few women down."

"What about the lady in the park?"

He shook his head. "Put that aside. It was a derelict. We can downgrade that investigation. Couple of homicide teams. No connection to the talk-show lady." He smiled. "I saw the reports. Prelim on the autopsy. Anatomically incompatible. You convinced me."

She did not react.

Then he said something nasty: "Look at it this way, you'll be able to pursue your long-running Stern mystery."

Chief Scott was not able to keep the delight out of his voice. He used the word *mystery* for a case that he believed held no engrossing secrets. He had made it clear that he believed that the "Stern Mystery" was a simple double homicide. A stale double homicide. The fact that the stolen items were valuable paintings was, in Chief Scott's view, a mere detail.

But even more important, he had removed Maggie from a politically sensitive case. Now she would not be dragging talk-show celebrities into a precinct house for questioning. And he wouldn't have to answer to the mayor and the police commissioner for her reckless behavior.

He cleared his throat. "And, look at it this way: You will be able to devote a lot more attention to the routine caseload, which is a heavy enough burden. Run over to Saks. Probably a case of mass hysteria. But run up after lunch."

She was dismissed. Still, she was disturbed by the loose ends and strange twists of the lady-in-the-park murder. So vicious. So calculated. And the odd planting of the purse.

It was while she was pondering these things that she bumped into the police flak, Marty Klein, at the watercooler.

"I hope you are not going to say I told you so," she said.

Maggie and Marty Klein had an interesting relationship. Without ever mentioning it, they recognized in each other certain qualities. It stemmed from the fact that both were essentially outsiders in an intensely inbred universe of career cops. She was shunned at the highest levels because she was an unbroken woman; he was excluded because he had never been a cop, never carried a gun, and was therefore suspected of being a journalist spy. Maggie and Marty Klein were never allowed to forget their diminished, excluded status.

Their exclusion had become apparent at one of the regular police dinner ceremonies when they sat side by side, and Marty Klein had made some funny, bitter remarks. A boy's fraternity, he said. He was still new at the job and allowed the disappointment to show. Maggie was consoling and told him that he should take the long view; the police department was no different than any other garden of snakes.

Now, as she emerged from the chief's office with her face pale and sagging, he recognized the conventional look of defeat. "You got snakebit," he said, shaking his head with his habitual melancholy.

"Right on the asp," she replied.

He nodded sympathetically. "I am glad that I'm not in your business," he said.

"Really? What's your trade?"

"I deal in concepts. Meaningless, abstract concepts. While you—poor devil—have to handle hard goods. Much better to deal with meaningless concepts."

They walked together to her cruiser. The streets in neighboring Chinatown were crowded and the atmosphere lent itself to exotic revelations. She felt a reckless spirit of defiance just walking out of headquarters with Marty Klein.

"You know, if you don't mind my saying . . ." She shook her head, urging him on. ". . . and this is a violation of my oath to say nothing specific, I think you underestimate these guys." He threw his head over his shoulders.

He shook his head and spoke in a conspiratorially low voice. "I always thought, you know, good cop, bad cop, that was the extent of their tactical imagination. But it's not. It's only one aspect of a chronic and fiendish psychological and intellectual trait. It is," he said, deepening his voice, "a sign of true intelligence." He tapped the side of his head. "I've found, since I've been in this job, that they have intuitive brilliance. They may not have read about the chaos theory, but they understand it. And the relationship of the citizen to the state. Apart from people in a think tank, they're about the only people who actually reflect on such matters!"

Maggie laughed. "This is one of your *concepts*, something you conceptualized. This is bullshit, am I right?"

"I'm not kidding," said Marty Klein. "Think about it. You can't get to run a complicated and dangerous system like this unless you possess something more than simple animal cunning. It's not just gimmicks and rough questioning in a back room. You have to imagine every possible impending danger, every source of looming trouble; you have to thwart ambitious subordinates. That's you, by the way. And you have to act dumb. Do you know why you have to act dumb?"

She shrugged. "Because they really are dumb?"

He shook his head. "Camouflage. Because they don't want you to know about the smart cop, dumb cop routine."

"Even him?"

He knew who she meant. "Especially him."

Dr. Judy Winner watched them carry out both women from Saks. She stood in the back of the crowd at the perfume counter, seeing it all from a green-and-yellow glaze, through eyes that would not focus, and misunderstood what was taking place. She leaned against the counter, afraid she might fall. Her chest pounded, she was dizzy.

At first, seeing all the police, she thought someone had been caught shoplifting. But all her second thoughts were personal. She concentrated on trying to breathe, to swallow, to stay upright. She thought that if she fell down she would never get up.

She tried to call out to a passing policeman for help, but she was torn between maintaining her public dignity and getting assistance. And, in the end, she was not certain that she had enough breath for an effective cry.

Finally, when the disturbance died down, she decided that she had to sit down. She was simply too weak to remain standing. If she sat, maybe she wouldn't feel so cramped and sweaty and would be able to shake off whatever it was that was making her so weak and breathless.

She headed for the exit, not realizing that she lurched like a drunk. Hector Bonilla watched her stagger across Forty-ninth Street. He followed her with his eyes as she entered the sanctuary of St. Patrick's Cathedral. He thought that she was probably another cardiac case, someone emotionally overwrought, physically affected by the twin misfortunes.

Then he was distracted, called back to help clean up the mess by his unfriendly supervisor. There were cotton swabs and needles and empty bandage wrappers on the floor. They couldn't depend on the cleaning staff to get it up quickly. This was Saks. Things had to be returned to normal. It was a business day.

In the resentment, Hector forgot about the lady reeling into the church.

Dr. Judy Winner had made her way into a side pew, where she collapsed. A priest returning from Saks saw her slide down onto the floor.

In that quiet urgent competence of his calling, the priest checked her vital signs, then called for another ambulance—this one from Cornell Medical Center.

The sound of the ambulance did not excite any unusual interest at Saks, where Hector Bonilla was waiting for his relief so that he could go to lunch and flirt with Maria. What was another ambulance? This was Midtown Manhattan—the home of colliding catastrophes.

EIGHTEEN

Peggy O'Neill walked more than a mile from Saks Fifth Avenue on Forty-ninth Street back to her hotel on Thirty-first Street. She was not bothered by what she had done. The bitter cold January air was strengthening. It was a stinging reminder of the days when she stood in the yard of her parochial school watching the frosty expressions on the faces of the priests and nuns, who were calculating the exact amount of distress that they could inflict on the rows of children shivering like twigs in the winter wind. God's bookkeepers, she thought.

That was the relentless catechism of her youth—pain and regret, sacrifice and submission. Evil was a concrete thing, the devil was an actual person, the plunge into hell was foreordained and inevitable.

"Now, Peggy, do you know what chaste means?"

To her, the nuns were always lifeless; behind the vocationally frozen smiles Peggy knew that they had nothing but contempt for the weak, loathsome creatures who would, sooner or later, succumb to the temptation of flesh. The nuns had taken their vows, they had sworn eternal opposition to all the secular and profane snares. How could they guess Peggy's greater, deeper misery? That she was a worldly creature, that she committed all the venal and mortal sins, engaged in every vice, and that, finally, it was a miserable flop—all the roaring pleasures of life were like ashes in her mouth. The transgressions were, in the end, worthless. There was no point in feeling guilt for committing unpleasant, disagreeable sins.

The streets of Manhattan on a cold winter day were marathons of racing pedestrians dashing for lights, dancing between cars, puffing out steam, retracting into their heavy coats like turtles. Peggy O'Neill felt no chill. She held her head high and marched at a soldier's pace toward the Gotham Hotel.

She felt nothing but the exhilaration of freedom. All the inhibitions were gone. Whatever was done was done by that person in the stranger's body. The lifelong task of showing soft compassion was lifted. She had mutated and hardened into something light and unbreakable. What a relief! She was absolved. Judy Winner, as well as all the other women (and Mickey, too), were victims of a process that began in a school courtyard a long time ago.

As she crossed Thirty-fourth Street, Peggy decided to stop and have a cup of tea in a diner on Lexington Avenue.

"Something with?" the Greek waiter demanded.

"Just tea," she replied with a sweet, angelic smile that sent him away muttering.

She drank the tea slowly and decided that her plans weren't done. Everything was moving along nicely and there was a goal at the end. She would know it when she reached it.

There was a man standing at the bulletproof reception window of the Gotham Hotel, shouting to the clerk. Peggy walked at a normal pace, trying not to attract attention. She could not help overhearing.

"It stinks!" cried the man.

He was a middle-aged man with a belly that bulged out of his shirt. His hair grew straight up and his hands were thick from whatever work he did. His clothing was wrinkled and cheap. The clerk on duty nodded and shrugged.

"I'm tellin' ya, 'at fuckin' smell, it ain't human!"

"Whatdaya want me to do?" shouted the clerk through the thick protective window. "Not all of the guests are up to your sanitary standards."

"You better do something! My friend says I should call nine-one-one. She says somethin's dead up there."

The clerk looked away, half bored, half ready to hunker down and deny the flak. He was one of those stubborn types who could simply refuse to budge. Obstinate for its own sake.

"You wanna call the cops, call the cops."

"I'm gonna! You think I fuckin' won't? Okay, gimme some change." He pushed a dollar bill through the narrow change opening at the bottom of the window.

"You know the rule, you gotta buy something."

The man glared for a moment. Then, "Okay, gimme a newspaper."

"We're out."

"Take the fuckin' money for a newspaper out of the dollar and gimme the change."

The clerk took the dollar bill and shoved four dimes back through the opening.

"What's that?" asked the man.

"I gave you the *Times*," replied the clerk.

"Gimme the fuckin' *Post*," snarled the man.

The clerk smiled and pushed back three more dimes and a nickle. Then, after the man dropped two dimes and a nickle into the broken phone, the clerk called out, "By the way, you don't need to deposit any money for nine-one-one calls."

The man gave him a hot look, but the clerk was sealed behind the bulletproof window. The man went into the phone booth in the lobby as Peggy climbed the stairs. Well, she thought, sooner or later, it was bound to come apart. Dousing the room with perfume couldn't disguise the smell.

She opened the door to the room carefully, making certain that she wasn't being watched. She gathered her things and stuffed them into two bags.

Then, making certain that there was nothing in the room to identify Mickey or herself, she checked the wound. Trying to inspect the body and the bleeding, she pushed Mickey, who started to roll off the bed. She grabbed him and pulled him back. It was an effort, and the stiffness of the corpse caused a small shudder.

She stood at the door and looked back into the room. Peggy had no sentiment, just practical thoughts. She tried to see the room through the eyes of the authorities. The police and the medical examiner would see a dead junkie with the needle still sticking out of his arm. They must find a few dozen dead junkies a week in the same condition. They would not look too closely, nor question too hard.

Not that she worried too much. All she needed was a little time. They would solve the case soon enough, but she required a modest distraction to buy that time.

The blood spilling out of the eye would be one more medical anomaly. By the time they performed an autopsy—if they even bothered—she would have done what she started out to do.

She closed the door behind her and slipped out of the hotel, past the indifferent clerk, who was still refusing to acknowledge that foul odors came under his sway.

NINETEEN

The face on the screen caught Maggie's eye. A group of detectives and uniformed officers were clustered around a television set in the corner of Manhattan North Detective Command in the Seventeenth Precinct. As she passed by, Lieutenant Maggie Van Zandt recognized the face of Judy Winner. Underneath the doctor's face was a bold title: BULLETIN.

Maggie stopped and pushed her way through the crowd and caught the tail end of the report.

". . . To recap, Dr. Judy Winner, noted psychologist, was struck down by a mysterious ailment today in Manhattan. She was rushed to New York Hospital–Cornell Medical Center, where she is in guarded condition. Her husband, talk-show host Kevin Grant, is now at her side."

A burst of chatter broke out among the detectives. Maggie pulled Chief Scott's aide, Sergeant Gil Player, aside.

"What gives?"

He shrugged. "She got sick. Probably about the ratings of her husband's show."

Maggie nodded, looked down, looked up, then asked casually, "She didn't get sick at Saks, did she?"

Sergeant Player laughed. "Always looking for a conspiracy," he said. "No, she got sick someplace else. Not Saks."

Nodding, Maggie spotted Sam, grabbed him under the arm, and left for her assignment at the chic Midtown store. "Maybe I can pick up a blouse while we're there," she said.

It took Maggie and Sam five minutes to make the half mile to Saks. The uniformed detail was still inside the store, clearing up last-minute items. A friendly lieutenant said that it was all wrapped up. No criminal act. A medical mystery, he said. Two women. One dead. The other in a coma. Probably both had contaminated eggs at the same coffee shop. The dead one was a fat woman in middle age. The other was younger, thinner. . . . They were both rich.

"You gotta be rich to hang around this store," said the uniformed lieutenant. "You see the prices?"

"Yeah, you should see my clothing bill," said Maggie. "Where'd they take 'em?"

"They were taken downtown to Bellevue. Listen. Happens."

He shrugged. A young old-timer, thought Maggie. He had a ten-year pin on his right breast pocket. Paunchy and thin-haired and streetwise, all before he hit forty. He would run some precinct some day soon, and probably do it well, judging by the quick cuts he made through the thickets of minutia, getting right to the chase.

"Talk to the kid on the door," he said, indicating Hector Bonilla.

"How come?"

"Well, he's got good eyes."

That was high praise, she thought, and she thanked the lieutenant.

Suddenly, Maggie's attention was deflected by the arrival of a howling flying circus of tactical units of police. The marked and unmarked cars screamed up to the store and parked at odd angles—the universal street symbol of a battlefield crisis. Uniformed units jumped out of vans and took up blocking positions around the store.

There were bomb-squad cars and dog units moving into the store.

The store had instantly become a frozen zone.

Then came the detectives, unmistakable in their size and pride, marching into the store like an elite unit of soldiers. They were followed by the comet and tail of high-ranking chiefs and their aides.

Camera crews and newspaper reporters were not far behind, blocked off and kept inside a barricaded holding pen.

"What gives?" she asked Marty Klein, who was trailing Chief Scott into Saks.

"This looks serious," he said grimly.

"What?"

"The two women," he said, stopping and turning and looking her squarely in the face. "We just got a report from the hospital. They were poisoned."

"Yeah, food poisoning."

"Yeah, yeah. Except the food was deliberately poisoned."

Chief Scott had taken the on-scene superior officers aside and was proclaiming his authority.

"He thinks this is a terrorist thing," whispered Klein.

"Really?"

"Pulled out War Plan B," said Klein, nodding. "Calling in reserves. Wants to summon an FBI response team. Wants to alert the Go Team from DC. It's like the World Trade Center."

"Hey, Marty, you think this is a terrorist thing?"

"I try not to think. I issue statements."

Maggie noticed Sam talking to customers, employees. Not formal interviews—just conversational chats. He had a knack for extracting nuggets quietly.

Chief Scott motioned to Maggie and Klein. He took them to the perfume counter, where he instructed them in their duties. She saw him blinking with excitement. He is enjoying this, she thought. The war leader thing, she decided.

"Listen, Klein, issue a statement. Tell those people"—he indicated the yapping gang of press—"that we are investigating a possible food-poisoning incident. Nothing more."

"That's all we know for certain," suggested Maggie.

"The doctors say different," said Chief Scott. "Some kind of boosted dose of digoxin. Those two women did not have heart conditions. Presumptive homicide. Maybe terrorist."

The ground floor of the store was filling up with cops with barking radios, uniformed men posted at exits, makeshift command posts of fancy tables and chairs. There was a low growl of police chatter—the implements and clamor of a full-blown emergency.

"You handle the store personnel," he said, turning to Maggie. Other groups would question the customers and passersby. Meanwhile, the bomb squad and chemical experts would go through the building as a precaution.

"I'll get a manager and someone who knows the architecture," offered Maggie. "To lead them."

"We're gonna set up a command post in a van on Fifth Avenue," Scott said. "The frozen zone will be ten square blocks."

"That's gonna tie up a lot of Midtown," offered Klein.

Scott didn't even answer, just glowered and went into a conference call with the mayor and the police commissioner. Maggie overheard him warning them away from the scene. "No, not for your safety," Scott said. "I know you want to be on the scene. But it is premature. If you show up here, it will elevate the scale of this thing. There will be panic."

He was right. She almost admired his cool efficiency. Maggie handed out assignments to working detectives. One team was to examine sales help on each floor. They were to direct their questions toward finding out if they saw anything unusual. If they spotted anyone unusual today, yesterday, or recently. Another team was to go over the managers. Another was to investigate the cleaning crews, and finally, she had the security group. She would work out of a desk in the lobby. Manage the cross-checking. Filter information.

Then she remembered what the uniformed lieutenant had said. The kid on the door had good eyes. She would start with him. Sam was already talking to the kid. He brought Hector to her French desk. Nice-looking kid, she thought. And not rattled. He asked if they could talk outside so that he could smoke a cigarette. Maggie said he could smoke in the store—the anti-smoking rule was suspended. He sat at the desk and held the unlit cigarette. The company rules were still too strong for him to violate.

His story was straightforward and clear and Hector had a good memory. Maggie pressed: Nothing unusual? Nothing odd?

"No, nothing."

Then Maggie made him go back to the beginning. He told her that he began work early, then snuck off and grabbed a smoke. "It was my break," he said. "But they don't like when you smoke in the store. Not even the bathroom."

He smiled. Nice smile, she thought. She saw what the lieutenant meant. The kid included explanations within his narrative.

"Then I'm standing at the door, you know, checking out the bums. That's half my job, keeping out the bums when it's cold. The merchandise detectors catch the shoplifters."

"You see these women come in?" asked Maggie.

"I wouldn't notice. Rich ladies coming into Saks, that's what we're here for."

"So what were you doing?"

"I was watching the bums. Oh, yeah, and the candy lady."

"Who?"

Sam and Maggie both asked at once.

"There was a lady passing out free samples," he said. "You know, from that store, what's the name? Chocolates. Ah, what the heck is the name?"

"Godiva?" suggested Sam.

"Yeah, that's it. Man, I wanted to grab a piece, but I didn't even know if she had authorization. I was gonna ask the supervisor but she was gone before I had a chance."

"What did she look like?" asked Maggie, who nodded to Sam, signaling him to take good notes.

"I don't know. Average. Brown coat. I noticed that. Matched the chocolate, I thought. But, tell you the truth, nothing struck me. Except maybe the hat. Very dumpy hat. Like a helmet."

Maggie interrupted, told Sam to run up to Godiva, which was three blocks north, and check out the Godiva lady. Bring her back.

"Tell me what you noticed, Hector," she pressed.

He shook his head. Shrugged. She saw the effort. "I really can't say what she looked like. She was like, ordinary, you know? Someone you see all the time."

"Didn't you think it was unusual that a woman was passing out chocolates at ten-thirty in the morning in thirty-degree weather?" asked Maggie.

He considered the question. "No," he said finally. "You should see the stuff that goes on outside here. Street performers. Peddlars with frostbite. People begging." He shook his head in admiration.

Then he talked her through the rest of the events. The lady inside the store tugging at his sleeve, the downed woman on the escalator stairs, the second victim on the third floor. The chaos of getting them both into ambulances quickly.

Maggie immediately phoned Scott, who took the details as confirmation of a terrorist attack. "This is how the poison was delivered," he shouted. He ordered Maggie to bring the security guard to the command post. He intended to match up the story with a forensic pathologist.

Just as Maggie started for the van, Sam returned.

"So?" asked Maggie.

"You know, Scott may be right. The people at Godiva do not send out people to give away free samples. Whoever was giving out Godiva chocolates, it wasn't someone hired by the store."

As they were walking north along Fifth Avenue, Hector remembered something. "The other lady."

"What other lady?"

"I saw this other lady who looked sick."

"What are you talking about?" asked Maggie.

"This other lady, at the perfume counter. A third lady. She looks gray and like she's ready to heave. She's leaning against the counter. I figure she's having an attack of shock. You know—sympathy. But then she heads for the exit. I was gonna go check on her, but my supervisor called me. Wanted me to clean up the mess. Then it slipped my mind."

"Did you see where she went?"

"Yeah, I watched her go into the church."

Maggie got on the cell phone and called the records man at the precinct.

"I got a question. Judy Winner. Where did she get sick?"

It only took a moment and then he was back on the line. "St. Patrick's Cathedral. Can't ask for a better place to get sick than that."

Scott was jugging cellular phones and standard phones and issuing a string of orders when Maggie and Sam came into the van with Hector. Hector repeated his story, his eyes bulging at the state-of-the-art equipment in the van. He was awed by the special units, wearing flak jackets and carrying automatic rifles, standing guard. Scott listened and nodded and sucked in the fact that someone handed out poison chocolates outside of Saks.

"Get me the mayor," he told Sergeant Player.

"Hold it a second," said Maggie, taking the chief aside. "This is important. The poisoning. There was another victim."

"Really?"

"Hector saw a third woman. She went across the street to St. Pat's. It was Judy Winner."

"God, this will really scare the shit out of people," said Scott, smacking the desk.

"But then it may not be a terrorist thing," said Maggie.

"What? What the hell are you talking about?"

"Maybe somebody was out to get Judy Winner. Not just an arbitrary terrorist attack."

"And they killed strangers?"

"Possible, boss!"

She could see that she was interrupting a pet theory. He was tapping his foot, one hand on the telephone. He wanted to issue the alert, order the federal Go Team into action, scare the shit out of the mayor.

"Lieutenant, okay! But that doesn't exclude a terrorist possibility, does it?"

"No, sir."

"So, my working hypothesis could be correct."

"Yes, sir."

"Fine. So now you are proposing another hypothesis. One which is, by my reckoning, remote, if not a little wacky."

"One has to pursue even the wackiest possibilities."

"Definitely. Now, under the direct orders of the commissioner, along with the approval of federal agencies, I am setting up working groups. Some groups will check out political terrorism as a possibility. Some will look into disgruntled employees. Another may examine the possibility of extraterrestrial extremists. I am putting you in charge of the group that will examine the possibility of an attack on a TV celebrity."

"Do I have a staff?"

"Sergeant Rosen."

"That's it?"

"Keep in touch."

TWENTY

Gary Lock's phone rang twice before the answering machine kicked in:

"This is a machine. It is designed to piss people off. So am I. Maybe you shouldn't even bother to leave a message."

Then the beep.

Kevin Grant had listened to his assistant's message a hundred times, and each time the beep was the most comforting, human part of the call. However, under the circumstances, he didn't know whom else to call. He wanted someone to "handle" things, spare him from the bumps and abrasions of dealing with the press—he really didn't want to talk to anyone. His senior production assistant was the closest thing to no one he could think of.

The hospital had given him a room so that he could duck the cameras and still be close to his sick wife. He sat on the high hospital bed surrounded by the digital monitors and saline hooks and the built-in blood-pressure cuffs. It was a modern off-white room with a Monet print on one wall and a clinical hospital TV set hanging down from a metallic arm over the bed. He hit the remote and found a newscaster repeating the bulletin that Dr. Judy Winner, wife of talk-show host Kevin Grant, had been rushed to Cornell Medical Center with a mysterious illness.

Kevin Grant jumped when the phone rang. He recognized the metallic clang of the voice of Judy's publicist, Mary Lester. Mary Lester tried to sound sympathetic, but he knew that she was calling from her cellular phone regarding the condition of an account, not a person.

"How is she?"

"We don't know."

He didn't know whom he meant by *we*, except perhaps the medical staff who were working on his wife.

"They said that she was delirious," he offered. "Incoherent."

"What the hell does that mean?" Mary Lester had a way of asking questions that backed people up against a wall.

"It means that she's delirious!"

"Start from the beginning. What the hell happened, Kevin?"

"Nobody knows. She was fine this morning. She went out to run some errands and then she just passed out."

"Was it a stroke? Heart attack?"

"No. They're running tests, but they said that it looks like some kind of reaction—maybe something she ate. I'm only guessing."

"Is she conscious?"

"I don't know."

"I'm coming over. Where are you?"

"Room 812. It's not necessary."

"It's necessary. I'll handle the fucking press. Hey, she's my baby!"

When he hung up, the phone rang again and he flinched again.

"This is the switchboard, Mr. Grant. I know you said that we shouldn't put through any calls, but Miss Lester . . . well, she insisted."

"It's okay. But from now on, ask me."

"I know. I should have thought of that."

Mary Lester must have been close by. It seemed that before he hung up on the switchboard operator, she was swinging through the door without bothering to knock.

"Nothing new?"

"Not lately."

"I got them to set up a pressroom. Sent out for cookies and coffee. They really don't know how to run things."

She made herself comfortable. She took off her coat, grabbed a chair, pulled over a rolling table, got the phone set up so that she could answer it—dug, in short, a kind of moveable public-relations campsite.

Kevin Grant was pacing now, gazing out of the window at the East River. A police launch was passing by, heading out to the mouth of the bay.

"God!" he said wistfully.

"I want the public-relations office,' she barked into the phone. "Now! Listen, who is this? . . . Okay, Phil, this is Mary Lester. I was just down there. Did I talk to you? Okay, I represent Dr. Judy Winner. Did you get that pressroom set up? . . . Not yet? You want this place crawling with Geraldo producers? You're gonna have camera crews in the fucking OR if you don't move your ass. Get that pressroom set up. Have someone at the front door of the hospital. This is important. More than one person. Catch them when they come in. Let reception escort the media crews to the pressroom. Take them by the hand. Make the pressroom close to the hospital entrance so the news crews don't get ambitious and wander off and steal drugs. You taking notes? I'm in 812 with Kevin Grant. Call me back when you have it under control. I'll dictate a release after we talk to the doctor. Better yet, get a doctor up here to brief us. And send some coffee, for Christ's sake, we're fading fast."

"You know," said Kevin Grant, staring out at the boat moving into the bay, "I really don't understand it. A week ago we were truly golden. Gossip columnists called to tell me jokes. How do they turn on you so fast?"

He looked back into the room and saw Mary Lester smoking. "I don't think you're allowed to smoke in here," he said.

She was annoyed. First, by the objection to the cigarette. But primarily by the disheartening recognition that Kevin Grant was, in the end, concerned mostly with Kevin Grant. She had thought that maybe when he was gazing out of the window he was daydreaming sentimentally about his wife. That would have been touching. She could have used that in some deep backgrounder with some magazine hack. But he wasn't thinking sentimental thoughts about Judy Winner. He was feeling sorry for himself.

Part of her felt a pang of sympathy for Judy Winner—not even her husband worried for her. She shook that off. Mary Lester always wanted to be the toughest guy in the room.

"No one is ever really at one with the press," she said. "Unless it's Buchanan. He's the exception. If you're a Nazi they'll treat you nice. But the press? Listen, I was a news hen for ten years. I kicked my way into every press conference they sent me to cover. You know who my biggest enemy was? The fucking press."

Kevin Grant had never paid much attention to Mary Lester. She had been just another attendant at court in his high-flying celebrity days; she was good at her job, but a little repulsive. Or maybe the job description called for repulsive people. Hard selling, kissing ass. Suddenly, he was struck by her deep, dark bitterness. In an almost depraved way, it made her physically attractive to him. He was drawn to these midforties career women who operated in obsessive overdrive, counting every calorie and draped in expensive clothing and dripping with venom. There was an impatience and self-absorption about them that he found irresistible. For the first time, he studied Mary Lester's face. There was a brittle, edgy quality to her appearance. He sensed a neediness that was strangely compensated for by his passivity.

There was a knock on the door, and then a tall, lean doctor came in, trailed by two junior physicians and a civilian.

"Mr. Grant?"

He nodded. The doctor stood straight as Kevin sank into the chair.

"I'm Martin Friedman, chief of medicine. This is Dr. Weeks, chief of toxicology, and Dr. Brooks, chief of internal medicine. I think you know Phil Martin, head of public relations."

They shook hands. The doctor looked inquisitively at Mary Lester, and Kevin Grant said that it was okay to speak, she was a member of the household staff.

"First, your wife is doing as well as can be expected. We have pumped her stomach and are hydrating her. We are also giving her an antibody called Digibind. From our preliminary examination, she's had a massive dose of a cardiac glycoside. The records show that she's had no history of heart problems, so we're a little puzzled by why she took something that is primarily used for congestive heart failure."

"I have no idea," Grant said.

These were people who were accustomed to delivering bad news, and they weighed and evaluated their audience as they progressed—being candid until they struck a nerve, then recanting a bit, and finally withdrawing into obfuscation.

"Well, we think that she's out of danger and stable."

"What does that mean?" asked Mary Lester in a soft, solicitous voice. She was a woman who was professionally devoted to hearing the worst.

"It means that we are monitoring all systems, hydrating her, and believe that unless there is some catastrophic recurrence, she'll be fine."

Mary Lester nodded. "Okay, we'll have to deal with this. I want you at the press conference." She was addressing the doctors. "All three of you."

"What press conference?" asked Dr. Friedman.

"We have to issue some sort of statement."

This was big-city medicine and they all understood, and began to preen, even here in the privacy of the room. Mary Lester looked at her watch. It was 3:10 in the afternoon. "There's a press conference scheduled at four. That'll give me time to work up a release and clear it with you. Meet me in the public-relations room at three-forty-five and we'll go over it. We'll hold it in the auditorium."

"That's assuming that there is no change in Dr. Winner's condition," offered the toxicologist as the doctors left the room.

"Of course," she said without a pause.

Mary Lester wrote out a release. It was short and said nothing, only that Judy Winner had some kind of attack and was recovering without complications.

"They'll ask about drugs," she said.

"She never took drugs," said Kevin. "Never. She worried about her health."

"Say that. They won't believe it, but asking will give them something to stick on the news."

Kevin Grant shivered. Then he noticed a glint in Mary Lester's eyes.

"Listen," she said urgently, "before we go down, can I ask a favor?"

"Depends," he said.

"This has to be between us."

"Fine."

Mary Lester's voice became lower, hoarse and desperate. "I need you for a second. I hit my Prozac limit and I'm a little uptight."

She motioned him toward the bathroom, and he felt all the hairs rise on his arms. He didn't know what was about to happen, but he was excited.

"Don't think of this as anything," she said, taking his hand, guiding him to the bathroom. "I just need to loosen up."

She had softened and grown dewy-eyed. He watched in amazement as she pulled up her skirt and began to rub herself with her right hand, pulling him along with her left hand. He did not resist hard, just followed along hypnotically. He noticed that they were now shielded from the front door, and it gave him a slight thrill. He was also jolted by her surprising strength. She took his hand and guided it down between her legs, under the fold of her panty hose, through the pubic jungle and directly onto the moist center of her need.

"Don't think of this as anything," she said breathlessly, imperatively. "It's really nothing."

Her voice was coming in tight little gasps and whimpers, and he found himself helpless and fascinated by her detached ecstatic distress. She needed him. She was desperate. It was, he told himself, an act of mercy. Harmless. His finger slipped into the gouge between her legs and he moved it rhythmically, along with her sympathetic motion.

She moaned and pleaded ceaselessly. "Please don't think . . . *uh, oh! Ohhhhh!*"

Unexpectedly, it was all over. He stood there flushed and bewildered. Mary Lester sighed once and got right back to business.

"Let's go," she said, straightening her skirt, gathering her press release, and looking calm.

TWENTY-ONE

By the time she returned to the station house from Saks, Maggie was just getting back her composure. It didn't help that she saw good reason for Chief Scott's disbelief. After all, it was probably a coincidence—Judy Winner was a victim in another act of random New York madness.

Someone handed out poison chocolate in front of Saks—what are the odds that it was an intentional attack on poor Judy Winner? What are the odds, she asked herself, that it was Peggy O'Neill? And what reason would Peggy O'Neill have for such loony behavior?

Maggie and Sam slumped down in her old office, deflated. As a distraction, and out of old eavesdropping habits, Maggie roamed through the stack of detective reports that lay on what used to be her own desk. It was an automatic and natural thing to do, since this was once her office and the objects on the desk had historically fallen under her dominion.

She came across an item that seemed to leech into her territory. At first, it seemed to be just another witness interview in the disappearance of Peggy O'Neill, reduced to the broken English of a police DD 5:

"Interviewed subject Janet Myers, who works for the public-relations firm of Pine & Cohen. Interview took place at subject's home—129 Apple Street in Brooklyn. Subject said that she had no knowledge of the O'Neill case. She works strictly for Dr. Judy Winner—wife of Kevin Grant. Subject said that the agency had been concerned about the disappearance of the O'Neill woman strictly because it might adversely affect their client. During the interview, the subject was called by Mary Lester, her boss, who informed subject that Dr. Judy Winner had been taken ill and was at New York Hospital. Subject told her boss that she would be available to help out during the emergency. Concluded interview and left a card with the request that Ms. Myers call the command if she thought of anything useful."

It was signed by Detective Jack Sanders, a clunky flatfoot, as Maggie remembered—not someone gifted with any clever or imaginative flair.

On a hunch, Maggie picked up the phone and punched in the number listed at the top of the DD 5. After identifying herself, she began to chat with Janet Myers. The woman hesitated and said that she would have to call back. Sensible person, thought Maggie. The woman didn't even take Maggie's phone number. She wanted to go through the precinct switchboard. That, too, impressed Maggie, who called downstairs and told the woman on the switchboard to put Janet Myers through to her old office. The call came back in a moment.

"I was reading your interview with Detective Sanders, and there were one or two points I wanted to clear up," she began. "When you saw her, did Dr. Judy appear ill to you?"

"Actually, I haven't seen her for a few days. She was doing that photo shoot for *TV guide.*"

"Right."

"But when I spoke to Mary—my boss—she didn't mention anything. Just that Dr. Judy was deeply involved in the photo shoot, so she must have been healthy yesterday."

"Right."

"I was very busy, myself, setting up an interview with someone from a magazine. A very pushy researcher. Wanted to see Dr. Judy on Saturday. Today. So I told her, Dr. Judy's weekends are sacred. She had appointments. Family. Whatever. She would not be available."

"Did you know this researcher?"

"No. Never met her before."

"Did you check her out? I mean, the reason I ask is that you were very careful with me. You didn't just accept my word for it that I was a detective. You called the precinct. Am I right?"

"Yes. You are right. I was careful."

"My question is, did you do the same thing with this researcher? Were you as careful?"

Maggie heard a slight hesitation. The woman was remembering, putting things together. That was one of Maggie's gifts: She could pose a question in such a way that the person on the other end was compelled to reassemble the scattered facts, turn them around so that they appeared in a new light. Often enough they arrived at unexpected, even uncomfortable conclusions when they tried the new twist. Which is what Janet Myers was doing.

"No, I wasn't as careful," Janet Myers said finally. "And it must have bothered me. Because you're right, I was very careful when you called. So my quick acceptance of this researcher must have registered as a mistake. Or maybe I'm just being paranoid."

"No. You're being smart. But why do you think it bothered you, I mean about this particular researcher? Was there something off about her?"

Again, a thoughtful hesitation. Then, "Yes, but I can't pin it down. Something. I don't know what."

"Well, let's start with the obvious. What did this woman look like?"

"Oh, I don't know. Middle-aged. Dumpy. A little unusual."

"How so?"

"Well, you know, magazine researchers are usually young. Bright. Very sharp. Keen, would be the word to describe them. A lot of energy. And very hip. They're all just out of the Ivy Leagues and all itching to break into big-time journalism."

"And this woman didn't look like that?"

"No." Janet Myers laughed. "Anything but. She was, as I say, dumpy. Had that defeated housewife look. And not very clever when it came to the rules and customs of journalism, if you know what I mean."

"No, I don't. You mean, she didn't know her business?"

"Right. Like very common terms of art were a little alien. Clips. Bio. Profile. I had the feeling she didn't know what I was talking about."

Maggie let that sink in. Then she popped another line of questioning: "Lemme ask you, did Dr. Winner have an appointment at Saks today?"

"Saks?"

"Yes. The department store. Did she have an appointment there today?"

"Well, as a matter of fact she did."

"Did you mention this to the researcher?"

Maggie heard a worried pause. The public-relations woman was calculating her liability.

"No," she said.

Maggie waited. In delicate questioning, she knew that it could help to allow time for a second thought. Like having someone make another try at a car's balky ignition.

"Yes," Janet Myers said eventually. "Now that I think about it, I was trying to avoid this researcher's attempts to get an interview on a weekend and so, yes, I did mention that Dr. Judy had some fitting at Saks. I thought that was specific enough to discourage any more attempts to bother the doctor."

"That makes sense. Is there anything else you mentioned?"

The hesitation was shorter. "Nooo. I don't think so."

"Anything personal? Habits. That sort of thing." Memories had to be prompted, coaxed along gently.

"Well, I pointed out that Dr. Judy liked to spend time with her husband. She needed the weekends to recharge her batteries. That's all. The woman kept pushing for a quick interview, but I was pretty firm, Lieutenant."

"Listen, we're all just fishing around here—you know? We don't even know what the hell we're looking for. Someone disappears like that woman from the talk show and it causes a big fuss. Then Dr. Judy getting sick. Coincidence. But it has to be checked out."

"You know, I also mentioned—I'm sure about this—that Dr. Judy volunteered in a food kitchen. I know I didn't tell her which one. I don't even know. Dr. Judy does it once a month or so, and it's been a few weeks, so I don't suppose there's any connection there."

"No," agreed Maggie.

"And Dr. Judy never made it to Saks," Janet Myers said hopefully. "She got sick before she even got there. So there's no connection, is there, between this researcher and Dr. Judy?"

"None."

Maggie was patient. She held the phone, listening to the breathing on the other end, knowing that the public-relations woman was grinding out details, trying to be helpful, trying even harder to justify her behavior. "Wait!" cried Janet Myers. "There was something else. Nothing, really. I happened to mention chocolate. You know, Dr. Judy has a real sweet tooth. Dark chocolates. Cannot resist them. And I mentioned it to this woman. You know? So I was thinking, just now, maybe she sent her a box of chocolates—as a gift, an icebreaker. Reporters do that when they're trying to get an interview. They send candy or flowers. Maybe she sent a box of chocolates and the candy was spoiled. You know what I mean? That could happen, couldn't it?"

When she listened to the detail about the dark chocolates, the hairs on Maggie's arms rose.

After filling in Sam, sending him to Brooklyn to firm up the interview with Janet Myers, handing him a blowup of the face of Peggy O'Neill, telling him to get everything down on paper with a signature, Maggie called the chief.

"Not now," he said. "We're trying to keep this off the air. We're really afraid of panic."

"Boss, I don't think this is a terrorist thing."

"You know that for certain?"

"I'm working on it."

"Look, I'm goin' on the air and telling people not to eat food off the streets. That sounds like a good idea, period! You want me to tell them it's okay to take candy from a stranger?"

"Not exactly. I just think there's another motive. It's not terrorism. Someone wanted to hurt Judy Winner."

"Who?"

"Mickey O'Neill."

"That was Mickey O'Neill giving out free chocolate in front of Saks?"

"No. Peggy."

"How'd he get her to do that?"

"I don't know."

There was a long pause. "You're way off base. But you bring me proof and we'll talk!"

It was just turning dark when Maggie pulled up to Manucci's Bar & Restaurant on Second Avenue near Eighty-first Street. It was the right spot because she saw a lot of tough-guy cars sprawled all over Second Avenue. Like bullies with their legs in the aisle. She watched a steady stream of sleek and beefy men dangling leggy blondes making their theatrical entrance into the bar. She trailed a group who walked the slow, insolent police glide into the room, making half-lidded turns to check out the house, nodding subtly to someone who nodded back just as subtly, then sent the blondes off to check the coats. They all performed the automatic hitch—patting their holsters.

"Hey, a party and you didn't ask me?" complained Maggie, grabbing Tommy Twist's hand. He pulled a cigar out of his youthful mouth and kissed her hand.

Tommy Twist's real name was Tommy Kidd, so he became, naturally, Kid Twist, and since there weren't enough people around who remembered Kid Twist, he became simply and appropriately Tommy Twist. That sounded about right.

Hard to believe that this baby-faced legend had only spent ten years on the job, Maggie thought. His name had been around forever. Some of the tales of Tommy Twist's wild courage, street moxy, and superhuman strength were actually true. She knew for a fact that he once lifted a car bare-handed and moved it into a no-parking zone so that a very unpopular sergeant would be eligible for a parking ticket.

And Tommy Twist had charms beyond strength. He was a true connoisseur of the full range of mankind—from cold killers to dishy celebrities. He counted heartless takeover despots and land developers who operated like wingwalkers among his companions. At his exclusive table in the most coveted mob restaurants in Manhattan, you could always find a selection of movie directors and authors, supermodels and rehabbed baseball stars, hookers and pimps. Anyone who lived on the front page of the daily tabloids was welcome at Tommy's table.

The one group you would not find was police superchiefs. They treated Tommy Twist with smoldering suspicion. The police brass were mystified by the fact that he had access to the secret files of the FBI, the National Security Agency, the CIA, the Mossad, and MI 5. They dismissed him as a charlatan and a thief. A first-grade detective who tossed around big money and dressed in two-thousand-dollar suits and wore a diamond wristwatch and dined at four-star restaurants and flew off to Paris in first class, according to all experience, had to be a crook.

However, they were never able to catch Tommy Twist committing an act of wrongdoing, in spite of the fact that when he was a serving detective, he was always trailed by an internal affairs and undercover team looking for dirt. The biggest secret that Tommy Twist hid was that he was, in fact, an honest man. He enjoyed the whiff of scandal because, he said, it increased his magic.

After he was shot bringing down a cop killer (a feat that enhanced his brilliant image among the line officers), he pensioned out and opened up a hugely successful private detective agency. It amused him that he was able to charge great fees to protect all those celebrities he protected for nothing when he was a civil servant.

But his heart was still on the job. Cops loved him because he defied the chiefs and got away with it. And there was another powerful catalyst: Every working cop knew that after retiring, he could boost his pension by going to work for Tommy Twist. So very few requests for information, assistance, or support went unanswered.

At his celebrated parties, Tommy always sat near the front, at a table that became a grand throne. In the amber light of the dim room he accepted the obeisance of the arrivals like a Mafia don. The exaggerated protocol was something that Tommy picked up from his mob friends. But he rose out of his chair for Maggie.

"Lieutenant fucking Maggie! Who said you weren't invited? You fucking wound me!" Tommy spoke, even when there wasn't eardrum-breaking music, at a foulmouthed roar. It was the natural enthusiasm of a fan. "It goes without saying—you're always welcome. The best-looking lieutenant in the whole fucking department. Don't I always say that?"

The attending chorus of hangers-on, bodyguards, and nifty women all echoed agreement.

"That's what I like about you, Tommy: You manage to kiss ass without making a girl drop her pants," she replied.

He held up her hand. "Does this look like your ass?"

The two twitchy models on Tommy's flanks giggled. A big former captain—now Tommy's personal bodyguard and flunky—smiled, which was as close to a show of human recognition as he could manage.

"Where the fuck is Sam?"

"He's chasing bad guys."

"Get that fucking bum to call me, willya?"

Tommy had once worked with Sergeant Sad Sam Rosen, and they had between them an improbable and genuine affection. More than once Tommy offered Sam a senior post in his growing business. Sam managed to turn him down without offending.

"Hey, Mags, give up that fucking day job and come be my partner," said Tommy, signaling a waiter to bring the tray of bloated steroid shrimps and to take drink orders. "I guarantee—you'll make more in a week . . ."

"I can't," she said. "My mission is to ruin a certain chief. I may need your help."

"Listen, I hear things," he said. "And I know you're way out on a fuckin' limb."

"Yeah, and I got no soldiers."

"Just call," said Tommy.

"Stand by. You may even have to leave the party."

He looked around, squinted, and then shrugged. "Just don't try to clean up my fuckin' speech."

TWENTY-TWO

Jerry Munk had the gentle stoop of a tall man. Not that he had reached abnormal, head-bumping height, but he was imbued with a deep-seated, self-deprecating humility that made him unwilling to call attention to himself. Often, as in this case, it had the opposite effect. As he entered Le Veau d'Or, his favorite French restaurant, on East Sixtieth Street, Robert, the owner, reacted with genuine pleasure.

"Ah! Bon soir, Doctor!"

He always called Jerry "Doctor." It cemented and bestowed a formal, titled legitimacy to the relationship.

As Jerry took off his coat and handed it to the hatcheck girl, Robert kept looking past him.

"She's meeting me here," Jerry explained to the restaurateur.

"Ah, so she is still out catching the evildoers?" suggested Robert, who had been in America for forty of his seventy years but still managed to retain his heavy French accent.

"No one is safe tonight, Robert," whispered Jerry, and the restaurant owner nodded knowingly.

"You are this evening intimate?"

Jerry looked up quickly.

Robert enlarged: "You wish a booth in the rear where you can speak privately, or do you wish to be in the main section where you can show off this excellent woman?"

Jerry laughed. "Both," he said. "As in most things in life, my friend, I want both. But, alas, also as in most things in life, I accept what I can get." He smiled and shrugged. The gesture contained the painful acknowledgment of a small piece of wisdom.

Robert nodded in sympathy.

"I shall sit at the bar and await what destiny has to offer."

"Very wise, monsieur. And I shall join you, if that is permitted."

Jerry held out his hand, palms up, offering the adjacent stool to the owner.

They spoke of small things—the price of living in Manhattan, the decline of pleasure—and then Robert leaned closer and took a liberty. "If I may ask a question?" he began.

Jerry shrugged. He could not imagine anything tactless from Robert.

"It does not worry you, Miss Maggie's . . . occupation?"

Jerry shook his head. It was a topic that was never far off the table. "She is very good at what she does," he said. "I was a newspaper guy for many years. I thought that it was important." He waved an arm in the air and shook his head. "It wasn't."

"You did not like the journalism?"

His head was bent over a glass of wine. "I did," he said. "Once. But no more. Like everything else, it's been poisoned." He sighed. "Celebrities. Fame. Greed." He shook his head. "Too, too much. I liked it when it was a quiet thing. No, what Maggie does is important."

There was a small fuss behind them, and Robert slipped quickly off the stool and rushed to the table where a customer had a complaint about a piece of undercooked tuna. Robert held himself with dignified scorn as he regarded the fish, then sent it back to the kitchen and tore up the check.

"The fish was prepared comme il faut," he whispered to Jerry when he resumed his place at the bar. "But you know, we have to be tolerant." He rolled his eyes. "I do not understand these people who order a piece of fish and then demand that it be turned into ashes."

"Actually, it is a fear of disease," explained Jerry. "It tastes better when it is a little pink inside, but is it safe? That is the quandry we parvenu vulgarians must invariably ask ourselves."

"Ah, monsieur le doctor, now we are at the heart of everything. You see, I believe that one has to risk a little something in life or else you might as well be dead. Not so? Take sex. You have heard of it? It is not a safe thing. It cannot be. In its most exquisite moment, life itself hangs by a slender thread. And yet there are people who demand safe, protected sex. I ask you, what the hell is that? Unless you are willing to die for sex you might as well do it with a magazine. *N'est-ce pas?*"

"That is all very well, Robert, but it's not the same thrill with fish. I just don't know if pink tuna is worth it."

"That's because you are not French," replied Robert with complete, unqualified conviction.

They smiled at each other. Robert enjoyed Jerry's company and admitted him into his exclusive circle of companions. The truth was that Robert didn't really enjoy running a restaurant. He was a free-thinking French intellectual whose tables served as a convenient platform for his daily philosophical ruminations. And he had a wide sweep of customers upon whom to exercise his opinions. They came down the two tiny sets of stairs and entered the almost secret room, whose walls were crowded with signs stolen from Paris boulevards and art deco mirrors, to exchange passionate convictions.

Robert dissected materialism with investment brokers, admired aesthetics with magazine publishers, deplored everything with idle rich anarchists. But above all, he prized the lady cop who, upon her first visit to his salon, left behind in her seat a live bullet. The ammunition that fell accidentally from her purse was, to Robert's inflamed Gallic imagination, an act of high graceful drama. It was as if she left a rose.

Afterward, Robert spoke to Maggie and Jerry as if they were experts in the field of existential danger and life's great theater. The stuff of the evening news and the daily newspapers had come to life at one of his tables.

He touched Jerry's arm. "This business about the lady in the park . . .," he started to ask.

Just then the front door flew open and Maggie stood there with her eyes aflame, her hair wild from the wind, her face flushed with emotion. She was pulling off her gloves and looking around for Jerry.

Seeing the aroused lieutenant, Robert leaped off the stool and as he passed Jerry, he whispered, "Tonight, my friend, you are in for the pink tuna!"

They were in the back of the restaurant, head to head, the food untouched between them. Only the complimentary bottle of Bordeaux was drained. From the bar, Robert watched with a mixture of sadness and interest. He would like to eavesdrop, but he knew better. Lieutenant Maggie was already agitated.

"You are . . . what? On vacation?" asked Jerry Munk.

She shrugged, shook her head. "No! No! He just wants me out of sight. Not prominent."

"Ahhh!"

"What the hell does that mean, 'Ahhh!'?"

"The literal translation is that I acknowledge this new state of improminence. I accept what you tell me and I tuck this information away carefully for future referral."

"You do?"

"I certainly do."

She picked up the wineglass and emptied it.

"You're an asshole," she said.

"I won't argue."

She shook her head. "I am perturbed. This Peggy O'Neill— where is she? Where is her ex-husband? What's going on?"

"It will emerge in time."

"What the hell does that mean?"

"I don't know." He was trying not to incite her.

"I know what you're thinking. You think I should go out there and pick a fight. You think I should crack this case and stuff the solution down his throat!"

"No. Not at all. I am a pacifist when it comes to waging losing wars for the sake of principle."

"Well, you can save your breath. I'm not gonna give him the satisfaction. If I had to solve this case, it would take unorthodox methods. Don't think I haven't thought of that. It's just what he wants. That schmuck is just itching to get my badge. But I could do it."

"I thought he wants to get into your pants?"

"He wants both," she said with archdignity. "He gets neither."

"Good for you."

"You think I'm right?"

"Of course. Go by the book."

"Well, you're mistaken. I'm completely wrong. I can't pull back just because it would cost me my job. What the hell's wrong with you? I'm a cop, for Christ's sake!"

He nodded. "I, myself, once worked for a very nervous Long Island newspaper, which refused at a crucial moment to print a column I considered vital to the preservation of the freedom and safety of Western civilization. You know something, for the life of me, I cannot even remember what that column was about."

She shook her head. "It's not the same thing."

"You're right."

"Stop saying that."

"What?"

"That I'm right. I'm not right. I'm wrong."

"Well, I happen to take issue with that because I think that you're absolutely right. But I don't want to fight about it."

He looked away, sipped some wine, knew where this was heading.

Outside, they heard the furious blend of advancing sirens.

Cops. Fire engines. Ambulances. Rescue. The emergency chorus of Manhattan.

She sat for a moment, quietly thinking. Then she opened her purse, picked up her cellular phone, and punched out Sam's number. "Meet me," she said. "Outside the Plaza. I wanna talk to Pudge and the Man again."

Then she leaned over and kissed Jerry Munk on the cheek. "I love it when you push me to do the right thing."

She left in the same blaze of emotion in which she had arrived.

"I think I just sent the pink tuna back to the kitchen," Jerry told the curious Robert.

TWENTY-THREE

Pudge and the Man Murphy were at the southeastern entrance of Central Park. They were about to have dinner when Maggie and Sam Rosen approached.

"Cold damn night," said the Man Murphy to the lieutenant and her sergeant.

They stood for a moment, waiting for a pair of civilians to pass.

"I need some help," said Maggie.

"Seems to me like we're on your payroll," said the Man.

"I need to find Nafume," she said.

Pudge and the Man looked at each other and laughed.

"What's funny? You guys just lock him up?"

"No, we just gave him twenty bucks," said Pudge. "Dinner money. He's down at Lex, getting some Chinese takeout."

"Twenty bucks?"

"He's picking something up for us, too," said the Man.

"You guys have become real foxhole buddies," said Sergeant Rosen.

They waited under the mounted statue of William Tecumseh Sherman, the Civil War general who sliced the Confederacy in two and burned down Atlanta. Finally they saw a ragged mass of material heading their way, dodging traffic to cross Fifth Avenue, holding two bags of takeout Chinese food. Nafume laid the bags down on the pedestal of the statue. He didn't seem surprised to find Maggie and Sam waiting, as well. Maggie didn't think that a man who lived Nafume's life could be surprised by much.

"Not enough food for everyone," he said to Maggie.

"It's okay," she said. "Not hungry. Go ahead and eat."

The two plainclothes officers and the ragged beggar arranged the food on plates. It steamed out into the cold night, and they dipped the plastic spoons into the pork fried rice with great, ravenous gusto. They sprinkled noodles and shrimp on the plastic plates and stuffed another spoonful of food in their mouths before they'd finished the first. Watching the excited and cheerful act of chewing and handling the hot food made Maggie and Sam jealous and colder.

When the first burning hunger had been satisfied, Maggie began to question Nafume gently.

"You know, Nafume, it's been my experience that when someone finds something in a garbage can—something, say, like a lady's purse—the first thing that they do is dip inside and get anything they can out."

"Why would I do that?" asked Nafume, contentedly gnawing on a sparerib.

"Well, in case anybody reclaimed it, for instance. That way you have separated the contents from the bag and have something left."

"When would I have a chance? Pudge and the Man were on me in a New York minute. What does that mean—New York minute?"

"It means that New Yorkers are by nature impatient and irritable. Like me. It means that we don't want to fuck around. Listen, there's no threat here. Just, like, I'm asking: Did you take anything out of the purse? Because you could have done that.

You had time. Pudge didn't get across the street for a minute.
More. Traffic."

"Yeah, but the wallet was still inside."

"You maybe didn't get a whack at that. Maybe you were sav-
ing it, or maybe you just grabbed and missed and came up with
something else."

Nafume dipped an egg roll into a cup of duck sauce. "They
searched me," he said.

"You could hide the Staten Island ferry inside there," said
Maggie, looking at the large, floppy layers of robes.

Nafume wagged his head uncertainly. He wasn't being diffi-
cult or uncooperative, merely feeling out Maggie to see how
much she knew. He cleaned off his hand with a bunch of wet
Handi Wipes and dropped it deep inside his robes. He felt
around in the folds and creases, looking for a pocket. When he
found it, he had trouble reclaiming his hand, which got caught
in the maze of the fabric. The stained and peeling hand emerged
finally holding triumphantly a book of matches.

"It coulda been," he said. "Things from everywhere. Some
scratch stuff maybe outta the purse. Maybe not. No money. I'da
felt money."

There were toothpicks and movie stubs and bus transfers
and a receipt for a bank withdrawal and a book of matches. The
matches bore the name of the Gotham Hotel on East Thirty-first
Street.

"There was one other thing," she said, her breath blowing
smoke in the cold. "Did you see a man?"

"What kind of man?"

"With her. Behind her. Accompanying her."

"If I'da seen a man, I woulda avoided that purse."

Maggie was puzzled. "Why?"

"I'da figured it for a sting."

Maggie was suddenly very tired. "Let's check this out tomorrow," she suggested. "It's late. Let's meet at Manhattan North
tomorrow at eight-thirty."

"Where's Manhattan North?" asked Nafume.

The others all looked at each other and smiled.

"No, Nafume," said Maggie. "Not you. You are a civilian. You are not a police officer. I meant a meeting of police officers."

"I'd make a great undercover."

George Service, the night manager at the Doral Inn on Lexington Avenue, watched the woman pacing back and forth; she was deciding whether to register, he thought. Not a hooker. A slightly ragged look—frayed around the edges—and she was very anxious. As if she was weighing the expense against the benefit. A housewife on the run, he decided.

"A single," she said, when she finally worked up enough courage and planted herself in front of the registration desk.

"That will be one-sixty-five per night plus tax; how will you pay?" asked George Service, reading the registration slip. "Mrs. O'Neill."

She handed her dead husband's MasterCard across the desk. The manager slid it through the sensor and made out a stub. She signed and he noticed that her hand trembled. Yeah, housewife on the run, and when her husband finds his credit card missing, he's gonna cancel, thought the manager. Better put the charge through as soon as possible.

Peggy O'Neill had a small overnight case. Inside were a few toiletries, a toothbrush, toothpaste, a Swiss army knife, a hamburger, and a diet cola. She tipped the bellman a dollar for showing her up to room 712 and then ate her meal at a small round table near a window looking out upon an alley. Then she collapsed on the bed. It smelled moist.

There was a movie playing on the television set. Something in black and white. Something from the forties with Humphrey Bogart, and she watched blindly, unable to follow the dialogue, unable to remember whether she had ever seen the movie before. Certain scenes looked familiar, but it could have been something suggestive—the recovered memory of similar sights and settings. Movies and stars no longer meant a thing to Peggy O'Neill. She had her task to perform, and all other considerations, all other frames of reference, all other cultural factors were ambient distractions. Noise.

She fell asleep in her clothes, listening to the sirens and trucks outside on the avenue.

TWENTY-FOUR

SUNDAY, JANUARY 15

The rattle of the telephone shook Maggie awake, out of her nightmare. In her dream she was facing a stoned killer, and her gun kept misfiring.

She picked up the receiver. "Please speak slowly—I am groggy and armed with a faulty weapon."

"Hey, Mags, get the fuck up!"

It took an instant for all the connections in her head to register. Then she was almost friendly. "Hello, Tommy. Give me a second to rinse out my head."

She dragged herself to the bathroom, brushed her teeth, took a long drink of water, then came back and fell on the bed. She lay next to the receiver. She didn't speak for a moment, but she could hear Tommy Twist screaming on the other end: "Where the fuck are you? Hey! Magster! Pick up the fucking phone!"

Softly, in a kind of intimate murmur, she said, "What time is it?"

"What the fuck time do ya think? It's fuckin' Sunday!"

She looked over at the radio clock. It said 5:20 A.M. That meant it was 6:20. She always shaved an hour off her day. Fooled her body into thinking that it went quicker. Almost like living in fake European time.

"You mind if I ask you a question, Tomster?"

"Ask a-fuckin'-way!"

"Have you ever uttered a complete sentence without using the Anglo-Saxon f-word?"

"No fuckin' way. What the fuck for?"

"Right. I see your point. So? How the fuck are you?"

"This asshole Scott, man, he's some fuckin' piece of work."

"I know you are leading up to something. Could we cut to the chase?"

"What the fuck does that mean? I never knew what that means. Cut to what chase? Who's chasing fuckin' who?"

"Tommy!"

"Yeah! Yeah! Well, Scottman is on the tube tellin' people not to fuckin' eat free stuff from people you don't know."

"Good idea."

"What about fuckin' restaurants? You think we're all on a first-name basis with every fuckin' chef?"

"It's harmless, Tommy!"

"Yeah, but I hear he's got the Joint Antiterrorist Task Force on red fuckin' alert."

She sighed. "It won't hurt them to stay on their toes. What about the other thing, that matter I asked you to check?"

Late Saturday night, Maggie called Tommy and asked him to use his unauthorized access to the use of Mickey O'Neill's credit cards. It was not something that she could do, given the privacy regulations and strict New York City Police Department rules, but Tommy went his own way in such matters and had no compunctions about reaching out to former colleagues who infiltrated the security departments of all the big corporations.

"Well, you know, my friend, you fuckin' owe me. Big time. This bozo O'Neill, he's been whackin' that MasterCard to the max."

Maggie sat up in bed. "Where? When?"

"Checkin' into hotels. Big fuckin' bill at this skid row on Thirty-first Street."

"When did that come through?"

"Last night. Went almost up to the max. How do you run up a six-hundred-dollar charge in a fleabag hotel?"

Sergeant Sam Rosen was already at the One Seven. She explained the developments, told him to meet her at the Gotham, and started to hang up.

"Wait!" she cried. "The stuff we took out of Nafume. Is it still there on my desk?"

"Yes," he said, and his voice cracked a little. "I'm looking at it. I'm looking at a book of matches from the Gotham Hotel."

They both felt a shiver.

It was still dark when Peggy O'Neill left the Doral hotel. There was no one on the front desk and the porter at work on the floor in the lobby didn't bother to look closely; he dismissed her as one more hooker fleeing the scene.

She had the Swiss army knife as well as the important telephone number in her new purse. The number and address were written on a card that Gary Lock had given her when she appeared on the show. Giving out his home number was meant to reassure the guest, demonstrating a willingness to reveal personal information.

Peggy had used the number to trace his address from the phone book that she brought to the hotel in her small overnight case. There were a few dozen Gary Locks in Manhattan. But the one that matched the home number written on the business card lived on East Forty-ninth Street.

That suited her nicely. She would have time for breakfast. She was surprisingly hungry.

She left her bag at the hotel and walked west to the Midtown Hilton on Avenue of the Americas and Fifty-third Street. The streets were empty and there were little plumes of smoke coming out of the manholes. She passed a few all-night revelers on their way home, some joggers running in the middle of the street, one or two Sunday workers, pushing rolling carts to the park, and the long string of homeless human beings coiled in the doorways or over steam vents. In the basement cafeteria there was a desultory breakfast trade at half past six in the morning. The waiter wore a dumb, indifferent expression that seemed appropriate to the hour.

"Eggs," she said. "Sunny-side up. Bacon. Well done. Orange juice. Coffee. Two orders of toast. French fries instead of home fries. And water."

The waiter appreciated an efficient, professional breakfast order and wrote it down quickly. He walked away without a word, merely a nod of approval. Peggy was famished. The hamburger last night and now the high-fat breakfast—they were all potential last meals in her eyes. She could eat whatever the hell she wanted now.

There was a leftover newspaper on the counter and she picked it up and read about some Washington political scandal. Scanning the rest of the paper, she found stories about three local stabbings at a teenage party, an infant abandoned in an alley, the fatal shooting of a doorman who refused to admit someone to a nightclub, and two Friday-the-thirteenth bad-luck sagas, but there was no mention of her own disappearance. The news had passed her by.

Well, she thought, as the eggs and bacon and potatoes slid around her plate, she would be back on the front page. She was, in fact, on the verge of being rediscovered.

She was finished with her food and her second cup of coffee before she was quite ready. She sat there for a moment, surprisingly happy. There was, in fact, nothing more to worry about. She was content, a feeling she had when she saw the end of a long and arduous set of assigned tasks.

With a happy sigh, she got up and, in the early morning frost, as the sun began to rise out of the Atlantic Ocean, she began strolling back across town, heading toward the light, in the direction of the apartment of Gary Lock. If she gauged her man right, she had plenty of time. He was not the type to be an early riser. Especially not on a Sunday morning.

She stopped at Rockefeller Center and gazed up at the towers, still freckled with Christmas decorations. She shook off a twinge of sentiment. There were days when she would watch on television the lighting ceremony of the tree looming over the Channel Gardens and weep. The sight of the festive horse-drawn carriages and the drivers in their top hats made her heart swell.

But there was no time for that now. She picked up the pace and headed east.

The night watch detective was still on duty at the Manhattan North Homicide Command when Maggie arrived at seven in the morning. He was finishing up a report that gave a large, sweeping impression of an uneventful night. The phones were still and there was a sleepy, dozing atmosphere in the room.

Maggie nodded at the detective on duty—Detective Haas something—and went straight to her old office. Maggie made herself at home and started going through the overnights.

During her reading of the detective reports, Sam came in bearing coffee and bagels.

"Called the boys," he said.

She nodded, knowing he meant Pudge and the Man.

"Told them to make it early."

Again, she nodded approval.

Then, while scavenging through the rest of the overnight reports, she found a detective report about a drug death at the Gotham Hotel.

The report was filled out at 11:00 P.M. Saturday night and forwarded routinely to Manhattan North Detectives.

"Investigated call about a corpse in room 315 at the Gotham Hotel. Dead man was found lying on the bed with a hypodermic needle still in his arm. According to the clerk, the dead man registered on Wednesday with an unknown female. The female had been seen several times going in and out of the hotel. Went out finally shortly before the body was discovered. The subject dead man had been seen only when they registered. Registration book showed that they registered under the names of Kevin and Judy Grant. No indication of foul play, other than the needle in the arm. Preliminary finding was that subject died of an accidental drug overdose. No further action taken."

She stood up. The report was signed by a third-grade detective who was "catching" and obviously couldn't wait to get home. The names didn't hit him with the same kick as they struck Maggie Van Zandt. She tried to suppress her excitement. Could be a coincidence, she told herself. Then she dismissed that possibility. This was a breakthrough moment. Only, she didn't quite grasp where the parts fit.

She jotted down some notes about the death at the Gotham, then called Tommy Kidd. She told him to meet her at the Gotham Hotel on East Thirty-first Street.

TWENTY-FIVE

At about eleven in the morning, the owner of Bari Fancy Fruits and Vegetables on the southeast corner of Second Avenue and Forty-ninth Street became aware of a woman standing outside in the cold. She was about a hundred feet down the block and appeared to be watching a building across Forty-ninth Street.

The greengrocer, Gino Bari, was setting out a stand of California apples when he first saw Peggy O'Neill. He looked up at the digital thermometer atop the *Daily News* building and saw that it read thirty-one degrees. The odd thing, he thought, was that the woman didn't seem influenced by the weather. He, himself, was wearing thermal layers and thick gloves and an old army pile cap to keep warm. She had what seemed to be a flimsy cloth winter coat and no hat. She simply stood there, watching the entrance to the house on the northeast corner.

He noticed her again twenty minutes later when he laid out another batch of Sunday newspapers. Same spot. Same stoic bearing. Like a sentry, he thought.

Gino, who considered himself an expert on human nature, began to speculate about the woman. She didn't fit into the surroundings. This was a reconfigured, tissue-thin, three-thousand-dollar-a-month studio-apartment neighborhood; it was sprinkled with upscale derelicts who kept the down-and-out drifters and claim-jumpers out of their territory. But this woman lived in Brooklyn or Queens or on Staten Island and shopped at a factory discount outlet and vacationed at Disney World. He was married to this kind of woman.

What was she doing lurking outside of an expensive apartment building on the trendy East Side of Manhattan on a bone-cold morning in January? Then he solved the mystery of Peggy O'Neill. She was a forsaken mother waiting to ambush a son or daughter who forgot to call home. That made a lot of sense.

Then he got busy and dismissed her from his mind. He didn't see her when Gary Lock emerged from his building and Peggy O'Neill came up behind him and whispered bluntly in his ear, "I am in trouble!"

Gary Lock jumped. He was a New Yorker now, and he had adjusted to the edgy native style, which was to always expect a street attack. He was relieved when he turned and found that he was facing a woman—he thought that he could handle a woman.

"It's you!" he said finally, looking around her, relieved. He feared a news-action ambush camera crew. He wasn't certain what he had done wrong, but he knew himself well enough to suspect the worst.

Her head was down and she spoke softly so that he had to lean closer to hear.

"I need help," she said.

"How did you find me?"

"You gave me your number."

He shook his head. He remembered. Usually, he gave out false numbers. But under the pressure of the impending show, he had given Peggy his real number. He didn't think she'd ever use it. Just handed it out, an insincere offering, to establish trust.

"I need help," Peggy O'Neill repeated. "I don't know who else to turn to. I'm afraid."

"We thought you were dead."

She shook her head.

"Could we go some place and talk?"

There was a coffee shop on Forty-fifth Street and they sat in a booth. He could use her, he thought. He ordered the brunch special, pancakes and sausage. Peggy had a cheeseburger and fries.

He noticed a muted excitement about her, which baffled him. He thought it would reveal itself and become part of the redemptive show.

"My ex-husband is going to kill me," she said simply. Her mouth was full of food, and Gary Lock was struck by the peculiar sight and sound of someone making such a desperate declaration through a mouth full of cheeseburger and potato.

"Mickey?"

She speared a bunch of french fries, which had been glued together by being cooked in deep fat. She dipped them in a puddle of ketchup and took them whole in her mouth. "Yes," she mumbled through the food.

"He's not going to kill you," Gary Lock said confidently.

Gary Lock was always reassuring people that he could work things out, that nothing was as bad as it seemed to the non-TV world. That was his job, to comfort the guests.

"He is. He swore that he would."

"Trust me," he said.

"I don't think you can appreciate how afraid I am," she said.

"We can handle it," he said with certainty.

They finished the food and the drinks and mopped up their faces. It had settled into a business brunch. "I feel responsible," he said. "I will put you up at a hotel. You will be safe at a hotel. I personally guarantee it."

"No," she said emphatically.

Then she told him how Mickey had come into her place of business—which is how she put it, "my place of business"—and dragged her out. He took her to a filthy hotel room in Manhattan where, for revenge, he had raped and beaten her for two days. She had escaped only after he passed out after a drug overdose.

"I'm not going into another hotel," she said.

"It won't be the same thing. This will be a nice hotel. He'll never be able to find you."

She shook her head.

He had a foolproof plan to protect her. He would put her on the air again. She wouldn't have to say a word. Someone else would narrate the story. And her story would arouse public sympathy and support. That would focus the blinding spotlight of TV exposure on her case. The police would be compelled to go out and find her ex-husband and subdue him. He would never be able to hurt her again.

"You know," he said solemnly, holding his hand up and wiggling his fingers for the check, "you have an obligation to prevent this from happening to another woman."

She shook her head. "I won't stay in a hotel."

"Just till the show tomorrow. Then we'll see that you can return to your normal life. With absolute protection."

"Not in a hotel. I am not going to go into another hotel. I'm too frightened."

She began to weep into her napkin.

"Tell you what," he said, after a long pause. "You can stay with me. At my apartment. You trust me, don't you?"

She looked up from her napkin. "If he finds out where I am, he'll come after me."

"How will he find out? I won't tell anyone," he said.

She reached across the table and touched his hand.

They were walking back to his apartment when she said, "But you can't put me on the show. Mr. Grant's wife is sick. I saw it on the news. He's not going to be able to do his show."

"She's better," he said. "Still in a coma, but beginning to react to stimuli. She's gonna make a full recovery. He'll do the show. He wants to do it. He needs the work to keep his mind busy.

It's a distraction from his troubles. And this will clear up a lot of his other concerns."

He stopped and turned to face Peggy O'Neill. "He's been very worried about you, you know. He will want to see that you are safe and well."

"But you won't tell him about me until we're on the show? You promised."

"No. I promised. Didn't I promise? You will be a surprise guest."

As they rolled downtown through the near-empty streets, Maggie was trying to fit things together.

"Why haven't we seen Mickey O'Neill?"

"Too smart?" suggested Sam.

"So why doesn't she make a run for it?"

"Too dumb?" suggested Sam.

She shook her head. "Judy and Kevin Grant! I don't believe in coincidence."

"What's going on, boss?" he asked.

"Hunches, Sam. Premonitions, suspicions, feelings. Too early to bring them out into the sunlight. They sound stupid. Humor me. Let's just keep this thing moving, one step at a time."

In response to Maggie's call, Tommy Kidd and two of his assistants were waiting outside of the Gotham Hotel. They were beefy and scowling men who had a deterrent effect on anyone who passed the hotel. Inside the dusty, dirty lobby, the clerk behind the bulletproof window glanced outside and, when he saw the three burly men hunched up in that aggressive, coiled manner, muttered to himself, "Cops."

Maggie rolled up, got out of the car, and nodded to Tommy Kidd. "Give me a minute," she said to Tommy. "I'll see if I can talk my way through this first."

Then she sent Sam up to the third floor and told him to canvas all the residents around room 315.

When she walked up to the bulletproof window of the

scrawny, half-bearded registration clerk and showed him her gold shield, he examined it with indifference.

"I guess you're not interested in the weekend special," he said.

"I need some information," she said.

"Yeah, well, we all need something."

Maggie looked around. There was no one else in the lobby. They smell cop in a place like this and clear out. It was a narrow lobby, partitioned off into safe and public areas. The cut and sagging couches were chained to the pipes. There was a moist smell of steam and something foul in the air. Maggie noticed the deep scratches on the bulletproof window in front of the desk clerk, as if someone standing outside had tested the strength of the glass.

"The guy who died yesterday," she said, still trying to be pleasant, as if she hadn't picked up the clerk's hostility. "Could you tell me something about him."

He shrugged. "He came in alive and went out in a body bag."

"Who was he?"

The clerk occupied himself with some papers on his desk. Maggie saw that he was doping out football bets. "Some junkie," he replied, shaking his head. "You'd be surprised, these people do not take care of themselves, healthwise. They have a very poor diet and they almost never exercise."

Sam came back down the stairs. He whispered in Maggie's ear, indicating the clerk. "A guy on three says that his name is Lenny and that he's a real prick."

"That's a surprise," she replied. Then she turned back to the clerk. "Listen, Lenny, this hasn't been working out between us, you know? I blame myself. What do you say we start over? Try to reclaim the magic. And I promise: I won't break your chops and you don't break mine."

He didn't answer right away. Allowed her appeal to sink in. "Suppose I tell you to go fuck yourself. Is that legal?"

Lenny smiled. It was a wicked smile that seemed to say that

Maggie had no real power over him. Whatever push she had, he was willing to take it.

She decided to break it off right then. There was no point elbowing him. Maggie had interrogated people like Lenny before. They didn't mind a little force. In fact, they enjoyed defying cops more than they cared about suffering.

Still, she tried one more approach. "You know, Len, I am not in the best of moods."

"You know what? Me, neither. I lost a paying customer last night. What's your excuse?"

"Listen . . . Ahhh, never mind."

"Have a really bad day, lady."

Maggie nodded and went outside and told Tommy Kidd she would be back in a few minutes.

"What do you need?" asked Tommy.

"My guy in there—the one behind the desk—his name is Lenny and he is singularly unhelpful. In fact, you could say that he's about the unfriendliest little creep since . . . I don't know. He reminds me of Koch. I'd like to convince him to be friendly. Cooperative. Without violating too many civil rights."

She headed to a coffee shop down the block.

One of Tommy's goons, a fireplug of a man, went in like an assault landing force and blocked the stairway. The second man, a former Special Forces assassin, was right behind the first; he reached under his coat, pulled out a heavy metal punch to break through the lock, and approached the door behind which the clerk watched in fascination. The former Special Forces man took aim with the stubby tool and splintered the wood around the lock with the first blow.

Tommy, too, was quick. He pushed open the office door and marched into the room, his Glock .9 millimeter out, pointing in the air in a conspicuous show of force. He pulled the clerk off the stool roughly and stood him up against a wall.

"Fuck you," said the clerk, flapping like a fish in Tommy's

grasp. He was thin-boned, Tommy thought, and would break easily. He had to be careful.

Tommy brought his knee up sharply, hitting the clerk squarely in the crotch. He saw the tears well up in the eyes of the clerk. He also saw something else—the clerk didn't mind. He turned and planted his elbow in the clerk's solar plexus, knocking out the wind and the insolence.

"You think we got limits, right?" said Tommy in a breathless whisper of pure menace. "You think we'll reach some point and stop, don't you? You fuckin' piece of shit! You are fucking with God, you moron!"

The clerk tried to spit, but Tommy's left hand took him around the throat until nothing went in or out. Just the gurgle and hiss of a leaky, desperate windpipe.

"You know how this is going to go down?" asked Tommy. He was talking into the clerk's ear.

Lenny still did not fully grasp his situation.

"See, you could be dead," said Tommy, pushing Lenny against the wall of the office, banging his head just enough to remind him that this was about violence and fucking him up. Tommy found a knob for a further interior room. He maneuvered the clerk into the back room. "Let's say that it was a robbery." Tommy was estimating the breaking point. This one, he thought, will require some convincing. "So you're dead." He whacked him in the kidneys. "It was a bad robbery. Who's gonna disagree? You're gone. We got a call and we found you dead. Shot with an untraceable gun. In any case, you're dead and there's one more open robbery homicide case that nobody gives a shit about. You beginning to get my drift, fuck-face?"

He was twisting both of Lenny's hands with one of his hands while holding a gun in Lenny's mouth with the other. The clerk felt the awesome power of a naturally strong man—someone who could kill him easily with one blow. Someone who would.

Lenny began to get nervous. He was alone in the back office with this powerful cop who had an automatic pistol stuck into his mouth. It wasn't just playful games with ropes and chains. This was life and death. The cop had that wild, fuck-it-all look in his eyes, and Lenny began to believe that these people were not going to be bluffed or stop at a beating. Out of his strangled throat, he managed to say, "Okay!"

Tommy felt a small twinge of regret. He would have enjoyed testing the limits. For both of their enjoyment, Tommy kneed him again, then picked him up like a puppet and put him back on the stool. The punk broke before he had a chance to really go to work.

When Maggie and Sam came back into the rear office, Lenny had his hands folded in his lap. He was trying to control the shaking.

"So, I hope I didn't miss anything important."

"Lenny here wants to help out. To do his civic duty," said Tommy.

"That right, Len?"

The clerk nodded.

"So who's the dead guy?" asked Maggie, handing him a container of coffee.

"He came in with a woman. Tuesday or Wednesday." He shook off the coffee. He didn't think he could swallow.

"Who was the woman? Was it her?"

She handed Lenny a photograph of Peggy O'Neill.

"Could be."

Tommy began to rise out of his chair. Maggie held up her hand.

"I really didn't notice. She wasn't anyone you'd notice, you know? Looks like her. But I can't swear."

Maggie nodded. He was telling the truth.

"You got a credit card?"

He hesitated, saw the instinct of Tommy Kidd to react, and nodded. "We always try to get an imprint of a credit card."

Maggie shook her head. "And you used it. Last night. When they carried poor Mr. O'Neill out in a body bag, you put through a six-hundred-twenty-four-dollar charge on his MasterCard. You did that knowing that poor Mr. O'Neill registered under the name of Grant."

"I never look at the names."

"The extra charge, was that for the funeral?"

He didn't answer.

"Gimme the receipt," she demanded.

He fumbled through his pockets and handed her the credit card slips. The name on the top was Michael X. O'Neill.

She was beginning to rethink the case. The relationship between Mickey O'Neill and his ex-wife was more complicated than she had first thought.

"Let's get to the morgue," she said. "I wanna see if that's really Mickey we got on a slab."

TWENTY-SIX

Before heading for the Manhattan morgue, Maggie called Pudge and the Man and told them to fetch Mel Carr. She needed someone who could identify Mickey O'Neill.

If that was Mickey O'Neill lying dead in the morgue, then there were certain assumptions Maggie would have to abandon. For one thing, it would establish conclusively that her ex-husband was no longer forcing Peggy O'Neill to commit crimes.

Therefore, if that was Peggy in front of Saks, and if she had been handing out poison candy, was she acting on her own? Did Mickey die later? Was she a villain, or simply a frightened victim lost in the great city?

Of course there was also another, trickier possibility—that the body in the morgue was not Mickey O'Neill. This was not unprecedented. After all, Maggie now knew that the dead woman in the park was not Peggy.

The flat and shabby New York City medical examiner's office on First Avenue and Thirty-first Street was almost reflectively depressing, considering what went on there. Apt, Maggie always thought, in its futile attempt to look modern and efficient. There was nothing stimulating about death.

Pudge was waiting for Maggie in the peeling, exhausted lobby.

"Where's Carr?" she asked.

"He wasn't feeling great," said Pudge. "The guy has a bad heart. The Man took him across the street to get him something to eat."

Maggie rang the bell, and an orderly came out from a rear office of the medical examiner's office. "I want a medical examiner," she said, showing her badge.

The orderly, who was holding a hamburger and a can of soda, had a half-lidded slowness. "The duty ME's at lunch," he said.

"Call him," she said. "Do it now. I'll be back in four minutes."

He stopped her and gave her the standard requisition form to view the remains of a cadaver. She filled it out, then ran across First Avenue and found Mel Carr digging into a turkey sandwich with a side of fries and a large diet Coke. Not the nutritional choice for a man with a bad heart, she thought.

"Wrap it up to go," she told the Man, then led Mel Carr back to the morgue.

"You know, I am not certain that I should be doing this," he said. "I have a bad heart."

"This won't take long, Mr. Carr," she said gently. "I promise not to tax your heart. We just have to know if this is Mickey O'Neill."

It took another hour for the assistant medical examiner to return from lunch. They sat in the office of the morgue, and Mel Carr—out of nerves—ate his sandwich and french fries. "I could have done this in the restaurant," he said.

Mel Carr was a heavyset man, and Maggie was not amused at witnessing the ground laying for his next heart attack. He struggled for air between large bites of food.

Finally, the AME appeared, wearing his fresh, starched white coat and a severe frown. He was a young doctor with the uncertain cockiness of having been recently awarded a medical degree. "Lieutenant," he called, and Maggie got up from the seat. He introduced himself. Dr. Glenn Ross, he said. It was three-thirty in the afternoon. An investigation that should have been moving like a bullet had bogged down in the mud of a dense bureaucracy.

Maggie took Mel Carr to the viewing window. She didn't think that he would react emotionally, but you never knew. She took a supporting position on his right and Sam sandwiched him in on the left. When the doctor opened the viewing curtain, it was like the opening of a small puppet theater. Only, behind the glass and inside the tiny theater, instead of plaster marionettes, there was a gurney with a dead body flat on top. The doctor lifted a cover sheet so that everyone could see clearly the face of the corpse.

"Oh, my!" whimpered Carr.

"Do you know who that is?" asked Maggie.

"I do. That's Mr. O'Neill," he said. His voice was shaky.

Maggie nodded.

"You are not to say a word about this," she instructed. Her voice conveyed the gravity of her message.

He agreed. He was far too confused to argue. Quickly now, she sent the lawyer home with Pudge and the Man, then took the doctor aside. "You know, Dr. Ross, I have the autopsy prelim and it says that this guy died of a probable drug overdose." She nodded at the man lying on the gurney.

The doctor walked back into the viewing room, and Maggie followed. He studied the man, who was in an advanced state of rigor mortis, for a moment. "Yes," he said finally, defensively. "He did have some other puncture wounds. And there was a needle in his arm."

"Did you do a gross examination?"

"Not me. There was another AME on duty at the time."

Maggie looked down at the sheet of paper. "The prelim says that there were no other wounds or injuries."

Dr. Ross looked over the notes on the preliminary autopsy that Maggie held and nodded. "That's what it says."

"But look at his right eye," she said.

The doctor bent in close. He shrugged.

"Now look at his left eye."

The doctor leaned over again and saw that the left eye had caved in. The indentation was plain. "That often happens in death," explained the doctor. "Especially violent death, as this would be, if it was an OD. Convulsions, automatic muscle reactions. A spasm could rupture a lot of vessels."

"Looks to me like a wound," persisted Maggie. "From a sharp instrument."

He turned and leaned in again. "Could be," he said unconvincingly. He saw the clear marks of a sharp intrusion. Something had pierced the cavity and then ricocheted off the bone and penetrated beyond, perhaps into the brain. It would take a real autopsy, cracking open the head, carving up the occipital lobe . . .

"You're right," he said finally, overcoming the inertial impulse to corroborate a lazy colleague. "It is a wound."

TWENTY-SEVEN

It started to turn dark while Gary Lock was still on the phone. He'd been busy all afternoon arranging for his "mystery guest" for tomorrow's talk show. Peggy hovered nearby, making certain that he didn't give away her identity.

"No, no, don't even ask," he told the executive producer, reached at his Greenwich, Connecticut, home. "Just trust me on this, okay? This is going to make us look good. Very good."

The executive producer in Connecticut, who felt a vast bitterness over the bad odor that Peggy O'Neill had brought down on the show, was not appeased by the assurance that the mystery guest would provide a happy ending to the sorry episode. He simply did not trust Gary Lock and said that he was ordering a backup guest, just in case.

"Bastards!" Gary Lock muttered after hanging up.

Peggy O'Neill didn't understand the underlying maneuvering and worry, but she sensed intuitively that interpersonal television skirmishing was no different from routine courtroom plea bargaining. The same sort of petty human drama involving power, envy, greed, and spite reigned. This perception boosted her determination.

"I'm gonna call Kevin," said Gary Lock.

She nodded.

Peggy only heard one end of the conversation: "How is she? . . . Well, that's a good sign. . . . I think we have to accept the doctor's word. . . . Listen, Kevin, she's a very strong lady and the fact that they are getting brain activity is a very, very positive thing. . . . I have no doubt that she's gonna be back soon yelling at me. . . . You know, you really should get some rest. You're not doing anybody any good just staying there. They can get in touch with you . . . Okay. Okay. . . . Now, I have a substitute host for tomorrow's show . . . No, you don't have to be there, you don't have to do the show. We can always have a guest host. Especially when everyone knows that you are undergoing a personal crisis. . . . I appreciate that, but are you certain that you can handle it, because I have an important surprise guest for the show? . . . No. No. No. Don't worry about Peggy O'Neill. I'm telling you . . . Trust me. I can guarantee that this is a very special guest and this show will go a long way to curing the problem we had . . ."

Peggy was standing over him as he spoke, disgusted by the insincerity.

He hung up and smiled at her, as if he were a parent and had engineered the solution to a tricky problem.

"It's all fixed," he said.

She waited, digesting all that she had heard, trying to fit together the two ends of the conversation. Then, finally, almost reassured that she was not being double-crossed, she said simply, "I'm hungry."

Gary's unlived-in studio apartment was crowded and dirty and had no uncluttered surfaces on which to eat. And there was nothing in the refrigerator except a few bottles of imported beer and a cold bottle of white wine. It was the apartment of an absentee tenant. The only time he spent there was to sleep or change clothing or pick up messages. "Let's go out to eat," she suggested.

He was astonished. What happened to all the terror and

dread of being recognized and tracked down by the brute maniac rapist of an ex-husband?

But then Gary Lock found a convenient and self-serving way of explaining the sudden change in her attitude. It was all due to his own comforting presence. He overcame Peggy O'Neill's fears and anxieties by the impact of his reassuring and clever steps. The woman knew that she was in good hands.

So they went to a fancy Chinese restaurant on Sixty-fifth Street off Broadway. It was an upscale Mandarin-style restaurant with layers of waiters and captains and maître d's in dinner jackets bearing leather-bound menus and a long wine list. It was padded and carpeted and there was a dragon motif.

Gary ordered a bottle of red wine and sizzling rice soup and braised duck and Hunan shrimp. They didn't speak much during the meal, but afterward, between the liquor and the food, they were lulled into a euphoric state of contentment.

"You really surprise me," he said.

She didn't answer. They were seated at a corner table in the back room, far from the next diners, secure in their conversation.

"I mean," he continued, "you were so different when you came onto the show. God, I remember how timid you were that first day, when you came in for the preinterview."

"So do I," she said.

"Look, we talk to five people a day, not counting the people we reject," he explained, leaning over, slurring his words a bit, softened by the wine into intimate revelations. "Of course I have to do it. Kevin can't handle the preshow interviews. He's too nervous. Too . . . too emotionally fragile to talk to guests before the show. Doesn't want to ruin the spontaneity."

"I see." She still had that dull edge in her voice.

"So I handle all that." He shrugged, as if to suggest that he hated it, that it was an ugly but necessary job. "I take the heat. You need a little heat, you know, for television. Sometimes, it becomes a little callous. Or, it seems a little callous. But if we didn't . . ."

He looked away, realizing that he was not getting through. Besides, he doubted that she understood the delicate nuances of what he was talking about. She was a civilian. And not a very bright one, at that.

Then, suddenly, changing pace, he burst out, "The food was good, wasn't it?"

She smiled. "Very tasty."

The captain brought the check in a little leather book. Gary took out his American Express card and the captain leaned over and whispered in his ear that they didn't accept that particular credit card.

Gary reached into his pocket, but he didn't have enough cash. "Look," he whispered to Peggy, "I left most of my cash back at the apartment. They don't take American Express. Do you happen to have any cash?"

Peggy handed the captain Mickey's old MasterCard.

In a moment, the captain was back, bending to speak discreetly into Peggy's ear.

"I'm afraid that the card was rejected," he said.

She flushed, fished out some twenties, took some from Gary, and handed them to the captain.

They walked out into a light snowfall, and Gary Lock could almost imagine that he was on a date. Except when he looked over at his dinner companion and saw the ordinary features and graceless slouch and lifeless look in her eyes.

"Boss?"

Maggie was standing in the doorway of her old office at the One Seven. Chief of Detectives Larry Scott was startled. He was in a frenzy over the public reaction to the poisoned candy warning. He was stuck with the tentative speculation from some doctors; he was alarmed at the thought that there was no terrorist.

The mayor, the police commissioner, the Federal Antiterrorism Task Force were all demanding confirmation or a backdown.

On the phone, the mayor told the commissioner to tell his

chief of detectives that he should not alarm the public. All the public officials were saying that there was no proof of deliberate poisonings. It made Larry Scott look a little silly. News commentators were starting to make fun of him, saying that everyone already knew not to take candy from strangers.

"It's snowing," said Maggie, shaking the moisture from her coat.

"I've been looking for you," he said with a kind of limp severity.

"And I've been looking for you."

The office was empty. Outside, squads of detectives in short sleeves were in the second stage of an investigation: writing reports; briefing newcomers; arranging for meals, sleep, and replacements.

The chief shook his head ruefully.

"Look, boss, I think I got a good case for making a link between the Saks poisonings and Peggy O'Neill."

He looked up, startled and annoyed. "No more wild theories," he said. "I bought your terrorist theory and look at the shit it's brought down."

"My terrorist theory?"

"Hector was your witness."

"Yeah, but I never said terrorist."

"You vouched for him."

"He sounded solid. He didn't say terrorist."

"What the hell did he say then? What the hell were you selling? I bought that shit!"

"I wasn't selling anything. Hector saw a lady handing out chocolate. The lady said she was from Godiva . . ."

The chief shook his head. He spoke with an exhausted voice. "He blew some smoke up your ass and you bought it. She never said Godiva. He thinks he saw a sign that said Godiva. It coulda been a candy knockoff thing, like fake Rolex watches."

"He saw Judy Winner nearly collapse. . . ."

He held a hand up like a claw and pushed the image away. "He can't identify her. He can't identify the woman outside the store. I read all the damn reports. You got me to go way out on a limb and left me there without a fucking ladder."

"Boss, they found Mickey O'Neill dead in a sleazy hotel room. . . ."

"I know. He had a playtime drug habit and did too much. I read the reports. What the hell does that mean?"

"It could mean that Peggy O'Neill killed him and tried to kill Judy Winner . . ."

"Hold it!" He sat bolt upright. "No more wacko pie-in-the-sky theories. It could also mean that she's scared shitless and afraid to come in. It could also mean that the business at the store was unconnected. It could further mean that Mickey O'Neill killed himself with an OD."

She had to admit—it could mean all of those things. But she knew that it didn't.

"I'm telling you, boss . . ."

"No," he said, standing up. "I'm telling you. Go home. Get some sleep. We'll have a tactical meeting tomorrow at noon. I cannot think anymore."

Outside, Sam Rosen was waiting. "The credit card was rejected at a Chinese restaurant on the West Side about an hour ago," he said.

"Tommy?" she asked.

Sam nodded. "Just called."

She said that she would make a run up to the restaurant and talk to the people there and then see that Kevin Grant had adequate protection. She wanted Sam to look in on Gary Lock. Those were the only two other potential targets on Peggy O'Neill's enemy list Maggie could think of.

Sad Sam Rosen rang the downstairs bell and waited for the voice. He was tired and cold and had no thought of danger. He was, in fact, completely off guard.

"Who is it?" said the voice on the intercom.

"It's Sergeant Rosen."

Peggy O'Neill looked anxious. Not frightened, but a heightened sense of concentration.

"Don't tell him that I'm here," she said, and Gary Lock nodded reluctantly. He didn't understand, but he accepted it. She was afraid of letting anyone know where she was hiding out.

She hid behind the screen in front of the kitchen. The policeman sat on a couch, his back to the kitchen screen, and Gary Lock sat on a chair, facing it.

"You know, there are certain developments in this disappearance of Peggy O'Neill and we are concerned about your safety," began Sad Sam Rosen.

"What are you talking about?"

"Peggy O'Neill. She's alive."

Gary Lock blinked. "What's that to me?"

"Well, frankly, we're not all that certain of her mental stability."

Gary started to look at the screen, detecting some movement. "Please tell me exactly what you mean," he said.

"You know, there have been some deaths. The attempt on Judy Winner. And then Mickey O'Neill, her ex-husband . . ."

"What about her ex-husband?"

"He's dead . . ."

That's all he managed to say. Sam saw the sudden frantic look in Gary Lock's eyes. He thought that the assistant producer was registering fear. He didn't connect it to an imminent threat.

Peggy crept out from behind the screen, tiptoed quietly behind the policeman, and brought down a full bottle of wine on his head.

The bottle crashed against his head with devastating effect, cracking his skull and causing an immediate rupture of several major blood vessels and a swelling that increased the pressure in his head and rendered him immediately unconscious.

Gary Lock was paralyzed with fear. He watched, frozen, as

Peggy O'Neill calmly stepped over the prone body of the police sergeant and removed Sam Rosen's service revolver from his shoulder holster. He saw Peggy's face, the hot, flushed glow, as she pointed the Glock .9 millimeter pistol at his forehead.

"Please! Please! Don't!"

"Okay," she said softly, sounding to Gary like the hiss of a cobra. "I won't kill you. But you take me into the studio tomorrow. You get me onto the set."

TWENTY-EIGHT

MONDAY, JANUARY 16

Gary Lock spent the night with his hands behind his back, bound by two of his $150 silk neckties. Peggy O'Neill sat across from him, in deep shadows, drifting in and out of a light sleep. She considered the possibility that he might make an attempt to break out, but sometime after midnight, she dismissed the idea.

Gary decided that question much earlier. He knew that he was incapable of an attack. Even when the time came to defend himself against murder, he didn't know if he'd be able to act. And he thought it would come to that.

It was an unavoidable consideration as he lay bound on the floor, listening to the gurgling, dying sounds coming out of the mouth of Sam Rosen. The strangling noises were a minor comfort; at least the policeman was still alive.

Beginning at six in the morning, his phone began to ring incessantly. The caller kept hanging up when the answering machine kicked in.

By eight in the morning, Peggy untied Gary Lock and they left the apartment together. She was afraid that the caller would quit trying to get through by phone and show up in person. Peggy had Sam Rosen's Glock .9 millimeter in a brown Lands' End shoulder bag that she took from Gary's desk. She was able to keep her hand inside the bag while it was slung over her shoulder. She walked half a step behind him so that she had a clear shot at his side.

"Do you think that Sergeant Rosen is okay?" he asked.

They were walking along Third Avenue, across from Bloomingdale's on Fifty-ninth Street, in the heart of upscale Manhattan. The early commuters were rushing to get to work.

"I think he was trying to talk," said Gary Lock.

"He's not in pain," she replied in a detached and scratchy voice.

Then she asked, "When can we get into the studio?"

He told her that by nine-thirty there would be a lull at the Global Television Network studio on West Sixty-seventh Street. The first audience of the day would have already left Studio A-4 after attending *The Eye Openers,* the show that featured Jerry King and Melanie Lowe, a popular pair of bickering morning talkers and slapstick artists. At that hour security would be lax, attention would drift, and he and Peggy O'Neill would not attract any attention as they arrived for *The Kevin Grant Show.*

They had breakfast in the street. It was cold and he was shivering, and he greedily gobbled a buttered bagel and drank the blistering coffee. Peggy was more deliberate, eating slowly, sipping delicately. He had suggested that they would be more comfortable in the corner cafeteria, but she said that he should not try to trick her; they would certainly be recognized in the cafeteria and then she would be forced to kill him and herself.

Afterward, when they passed a policeman, he averted his eyes as if he were the criminal.

Peggy noticed. He had become her ally.

When they entered the network headquarters, Gary Lock tried to duplicate his usual cocky attitude. "She's with me," he said to the receptionist, flinging a thumb over his shoulder. The woman didn't even look up from her crossword puzzle.

They went straight to his office, where they remained. From behind his locked door he answered the questions from the stage manager and director about the programming schedule.

At eleven, he had to open the door for Kevin Grant. The star of the show nodded briefly at Peggy O'Neill. She didn't register in his memory. The woman he remembered was broken, defeated, and at the mercy of life's tides. The talk-show host looked haggard and said that his wife was improving—at least according to the doctors.

"You know, you should get some rest, too," he said to Gary Lock. "You look like you haven't slept for a month." He patted his senior production assistant on the shoulder.

Then he excused himself and went to get a cup of coffee and to put on his makeup. They would discuss the day's show when he was done. He nodded again to Peggy when he left.

After grabbing a few hours of sleep, Maggie called Kevin Grant. He again assured her that he was safe. When she asked about Gary Lock, he said he had just left his office and that he was fine, as well. He had not seen Sam Rosen.

Maggie was in a controlled frenzy, not having heard from her sidekick. Somewhere between the precinct command and Gary Lock's apartment, Sergeant Sad Sam Rosen dropped off of the radar.

She found the show's executive producer in his limousine driving in from Connecticut. Paul Potito said that he had spoken to Gary Lock the previous evening and that Gary had promised to produce a mystery guest who would cleanse the show of any bad reputation from the Peggy O'Neill incident.

Maggie's suspicions were aroused.

Then she called Pudge and the Man and told them to meet her at the studio. When she got there, she used her badge and forced her way onto the soundstage. There was a preshow warm-up, and a well-pancaked announcer was telling the audience that they were about to witness a socially useful show. They should all be proud to be a part of it. This was not just another talk show. Kevin Grant dealt with real issues.

There was a heartfelt burst of applause from the few score tourists and studio regulars in the audience.

On the stage a bright light focused attention on the center of a large blue curtain. After a long hush, with blinking lights that announced that they were on the air, came a trumpet fanfare, and the curtain rose. The cameras came to life, and Maggie saw Kevin Grant sitting on a bar stool at the center of the stage, his face set in pain. To his right sat Gary Lock, with his hands folded in his lap and a distant, lost look on his face. To the far right, and at an odd angle, sat Peggy O'Neill, her face shielded from inspection. In her lap was her purse. Her right hand was inside her purse. Maggie felt an unfocused tingle of danger.

Kevin Grant began in his sober television voice: "Good day, ladies and gentlemen. We have a special show for you today. Last week we ran a show about spousal abuse. One of our guests was Peggy O'Neill. We think that we may have done some damage with that show—something that we never want to do—and today Peggy O'Neill has returned to bring us up-to-date. Welcome to today's show."

Peggy didn't speak.

Kevin Grant plunged ahead. "You know, the theme that we attempted to deal with last was spousal abuse. How to deal with it. How to recognize it. Peggy, your husband was abusive."

"That's right."

There was a smoky quality to her voice.

"And furthermore, he cheated on you."

"That's right."

"Now, on last week's show, you said that the faithlessness on his part was so bad that in order to even the score, you cheated on him."

There was a sudden and thick quiet in the studio.

"That's what I said," she replied.

"But that's not true."

"No."

"So then, if I may ask, why did you say it?"

"They told me to say it."

"They?"

Maggie saw Peggy push her handbag in the direction of Gary Lock. Her hand was still inside. "Tell them," she ordered.

The assistant producer identified on screen jumped, rousing himself from his sluggishness.

"It was my idea," he said quickly. "I suggested that Peggy O'Neill say that she had an affair to get even with her ex-husband."

There was a long pause, a marshalling of information.

"And why did you do that?" asked Kevin Grant finally, directing the question at the now alert Gary Lock.

"I thought it would make for a more dramatic show."

Peggy leaned toward him with a fierce look. "You told me that I would get even with him if I said that. You told me that I would do a service for women!"

"That's right," he said.

"So you didn't cheat on your husband as you said last week," said Kevin Grant, the moderator, interjecting himself as the voice of reason.

"No. I never did."

"I told her to embellish the story, Kevin," said Gary Lock, who looked to Maggie to be on the verge of tears. "It was my idea. I am to blame."

The stage manager and the director were standing near the main camera for a two shot. "What's going on here?" whispered the director.

"I don't know," said the stage manager, "but it's a helluva show."

"Do I cut them off?"

"Are you nuts?"

On the stage, Peggy never looked at the camera. Kevin Grant had a pasty, terrified expression. Gary Lock was trembling.

"And this changed your life?" asked Kevin Grant.

"It ended my life."

Some took that for a figure of speech.

The camera operators looked at each other. The director punched his microphone to the star's earpiece. "What's going on?"

Turning to his guest, Kevin Grant said, "Ladies and gentlemen, it seems pretty clear that we made a terrible mistake."

Peggy O'Neill shook her head. She looked up and Maggie could see clearly that her eyes burned with savage intensity. "You can't just say that you made a mistake. It's a little more than a mistake! Do you think that what happened to your wife was a mistake?"

There was a shocked intake of air in the audience. Some members of the audience cried out in chorus, "Shame!" Peggy had overshot the boundary of what was acceptable on television.

Within the viewing area, there was a gathering of a larger and larger mesmerized audience, as people within range summoned others to witness this strange, puzzling event on television. At the One Seven, Chief Scott sat staring at the television set in a cluster of bug-eyed detectives. "Get some people down to that studio," he ordered Sergeant Player. "Quick."

At City Hall, Mayor Sal Pilazzo watched with his staff in the secretaries' section of the executive wing. He was, like everyone else, dumbstruck.

At One Police Plaza, Police Commissioner Bradford Rogers stood with Marty Klein in paralyzed astonishment.

All over the city, the hushed and growing audience watched *The Kevin Grant Show* with a confusing mixture of fascination and disbelief.

Maggie knew that Peggy O'Neill had a gun in the shoulder bag. All of her police training told her so. The woman displayed an obvious power swagger from her perch on the stage; she seemed to be the complete master of the situation, and Kevin Grant and Gary Lock, two television professionals—men who would ordinarily have had her dragged off the stage by security guards—were slavishly obedient. And there was that other thing—instinct.

Maggie also grasped that time was running out; they were approaching some finite point at which she would have to act to protect lives.

"We're going to skip our first commercial," said Kevin Grant, "so that we can continue this conversation with Peggy O'Neill. You were saying, Miss O'Neill, how the show impacted you."

"Yes, my ex-husband watched the show and he tried to kill me. . . ."

"You were divorced, as I recall."

Maggie whispered to Pudge, "Get backup." Then she sent the Man Murphy to block Peggy's retreat. She whispered, "Don't make a move until you get a signal from me."

She checked her own gun, made certain it was loaded and that the action was working, and tucked it behind her, in the waistband of her skirt. Then she simply boldly walked out onto the set. It froze everyone. She took a spot behind Kevin Grant so that Peggy would not feel threatened. No one was on her flank.

Peggy O'Neill still had everyone within range. She maneuvered the shoulder bag so that it wavered between Maggie, Kevin Grant, and Gary Lock.

"We haven't met," said Maggie. "I'm Lieutenant Van Zandt."

"I know about you," said Peggy.

"You have been through a terrible ordeal and may I say that we are well aware of the history. How did you manage to get away from your ex-husband?"

Maggie understood the technique of talking to someone with a gun. There is a kind of babble used in hostage situations in which the authorities attempt to keep the conversation going by a steady stream of sympathetic chatter.

"I escaped. He fell asleep."

Maggie kept her talking, but she saw the hand emerge from the shoulder bag and there was an automatic pistol in Peggy's hand.

"Why don't you tell me what happened," said Maggie calmly.

"Tell you what happened?" Peggy's eyes were loose in her head, whirling around the set. The gun was out in the open, wandering back and forth, as if looking for a victim.

Maggie bent over, so that she could hear better. Suddenly, she grabbed Kevin Grant roughly behind the neck and by the waist—getting a good purchase on his center of gravity—and, with a great shove, pushed him off the set, out of the line of fire. He stumbled for an instant, caught by the microphone wires. But he kicked himself free and fled into the darkness.

Just as Peggy turned to aim at Grant, Gary Lock stood up. Maggie grabbed Gary's arm and pushed him toward the dark. He started to run, and Peggy raised her gun. "Don't!" cried Maggie, reaching behind to get her own gun.

Gary Lock thought that Maggie was yelling at him and he froze on the stage. It was just long enough for Peggy to turn away from her primary target, Grant, and fire one bullet into Lock's back. In the same instant, Maggie dropped to her knee and squeezed off four rounds, which hit all the vital organs in Peggy O'Neill's torso. Running in from the opposite direction, the Man Murphy put two more slugs into Peggy's dead body.

The live show was seen by several local stations who took the feed in real time. They witnessed the drama from Gary Lock's confession to his execution. And then the screen went black. There were some viewers, thinking that they had stumbled onto a daytime drama, who switched it off because it lacked verisimilitude.

EPILOGUE

There was, in the aftermath of the talk-show bloodbath, an attempt for everyone to reach a kind of safety. The events televised live were so shocking and disturbing, the implications so destructive to the public tranquility, that all parties headed for some kind of shelter.

And so they all agreed that Peggy O'Neill had been deeply unhinged and that it was, at best, a tragic misunderstanding.

There were, of course, some few who blamed the incendiary effects of television. This became a hot talk-show topic.

Kevin Grant and his wife, Dr. Judy Winner, started their own talk show, which became a wildly popular syndicated success. It was dedicated to the memory of Gary Lock. Each show had his name at the end of the final credits.

Chief Larry Scott was given full credit for masterminding the brilliant solution to the Saks mystery, as well as planning the trap for Peggy O'Neill. "She was enamored of television fame," he explained on one of the serious Sunday news programs. "I knew that the only way to lure her out of hiding was to arrange for an appearance on Kevin Grant's show."

Pudge Keene and the Man Murphy were promoted to detective and placed under Larry Scott's command, where—under Maggie Van Zandt's advice—they never spoke of their true beliefs about the proper blame for the talk-show calamity.

Nafume Benjamin was taken under the wing of a foundation. He returned to school and reentered the mainstream of American business life.

When they found Sam Rosen on the floor of Gary Lock's apartment, he was near death. The wounds to his head were profound. He was spared some emotional suffering by short-term memory loss. When Maggie went to see him in the neurological ward of New York Hospital a week later, she was afraid that she would find a vegetable instead of her old friend.

"How are you?" she asked gently.

She couldn't hear his answer. He beckoned and she lowered her head.

"That's it for me," he whispered. "From now on, I stick to soft drinks. Wine'll kill you."

Maggie laughed so hard that she cried. That night when she told Jerry, she just wept. He had never seen her cry.

"We should go to Europe," she said finally.

"Why? Didn't we just come back?"

"I want to go back and talk to the people in Avignon again."

"This is about the Sterns?"

"Manny and Lydia. It bothers me. You take a case and you look at it and you think you know what you're looking at. But you don't. Turn it around a little and you got a whole new picture."

"Now you're talking about Peggy O'Neill."

"I was very slow."

"But you got her."

They were sitting dreamily among the packing crates and rolled-up rugs in her new apartment. "There is a cop in Florence who faxed me some leads about the paintings stolen from the

Sterns' apartment. He heard of a Monet that had been sold by a shady dealer off of the Ponte Vecchio. Came from Avignon. I gotta go talk to this guy."

"You just don't wanna unpack."

"That, too."

Finally he said, "You know, you weren't that close to Manny Stern. He was a lawyer. You knew him from court. What's the big deal?"

"He was murdered! He and his wife. I'm a cop, for Christ's sake!"

"Can you get the time off?"

"Scott will give me the time."

"Or else?"

"Or else!"